Piccadilly Circus

When a group of former British colonialists retire to a sleepy Portuguese village, all hell breaks loose. They take over 'Millionaire Hill' and unleash the loose morals and naughty behavior which would have earned them nothing but scorn back home.

As transplanted expatriates living like kings and queens in an impoverished country, they feel perfectly entitled to drink away their days and lust away their nights, always pining away for the good old days of their youth, when the British Empire was still a power. The sudden outbreak of the Falklands War revives their patriotism and self-respect briefly but, in the end, the war becomes a powerful metaphor for the decadent, less relevant empire that they have created. With nothing but money and time on their hands, they entertain themselves in one debauchery after another. Trouble finds them around every corner; misadventure becomes their only companion.

Only one honorable Englishman manages to stand head and shoulders above the moral chaos all around him. Copper Jack is a voice of reason among the irrational. He is a throwback character to a better time and place. Copper's tempestuous marriage to Tookie Jack is his only tragic flaw and it brings him to the brink of self-destruction along with his fellow countrymen. In the end, *Piccadilly Circus* is first and foremost a literary love story, but the novel is also a powerful reminder of life's lessons and that love alone is not always enough.

First published in Great Britain in 2013 by U P Publications Ltd
Head Office: 25 Bedford Street, Peterborough, UK. PE1 4DN

Front Picture Design copyright © Mike Peers 2013
Cover Design copyright © U P Publications 2013

A CIP Catalogue record of this book is available from the British Library

ISBN 978-1908135339
9 2 5 7 0 8 6 4 3 1

Also published for Kindle by U P Publications under

ISBN 978-1908135346

FIRST PAPERBACK EDITION

Published by U P Publications Ltd
Printed in England by The Lightning Source Group

www.jamesallenmitchell.com
www.uppublications.ltd.uk

PICCADILLY CIRCUS

James Allen Mitchell

U P Publications
2013

Dedicated to Jack

Good men, the last wave by, crying how bright
Their frail deeds might have danced into a green bay.
Dylan Thomas

Prologue

Conquerors lost interest and always moved on.

Only the Moors lingered long enough to title this hundred-mile stretch of Portuguese coastline '*Al-Gharb*', to sabotage the architecture with an occasional grotesque-looking castle, to leave behind lean, leathery-skinned children with suspicious eyes.

From Sagres to Monte Gordo, it was a country of transient conquerors who raped her women and left them behind.

Today, retired English colonialists clutter her shores sipping gin and tonics beneath colored parasols. They fancy the Algarve's nearness to the equator and the extraordinary fullness of her moon gives them license to carry on as they please. Something to do with the blood running hot and the moon relaxing their deepest boarding-school inhibitions with a gentle tug of the tide…

1

Amen and Serve the Gin

Bed and breakfast was served six days a week. On the Sabbath, a day for miracles, Casa Bodega transformed into an Anglican church. Sun shimmered against the white-washed façade of the winery as it had for centuries. Instead of Portuguese peasants, former English colonialists crowded today through the heavy fortress-like doors.

"Marvelous! Marvelous!" Bilkington Bustle declared as he jostled shoulders with his fellow countrymen in his haste to get a drink. He knew the pub would close shortly on Sunday morning to become the church pulpit. "Marvelous! Marvelous!" he repeated, feeling no need to elaborate.

"Couldn't agree more," someone answered.

"Absolutely, I'm sure," another voice chimed in.

"Isn't it so," everyone seemed to agree, because it was marvelous. A thousand miles from the United Kingdom and several decades after the last Great War, a memorial church service commemorating the famous 'Battle of Britain' attracted even dedicated Sunday morning golfers like Bilkington Bustle.

Today, he and his British brethren came to the bodega in droves to re-live the war once more. This time the congregation would rely on the fading memory of one of the last surviving members of 'the Few', a legendary handful of Royal Air Force pilots who were all that stood between the Mother Country and extinction when the hordes of German Messerschmitts filled the beloved skies of London during World War II.

The surviving pilots, the 'fewer' today, vegetate away in rest homes for the most part, having flown one too many missions in their day. Pilot Officer

Winkie, for example, had returned from battle often enough to cover himself in glory before winding up in a loony bin near Cornwall soon after the war. He'd been only a passenger today on the 727 airliner that flew him to the distant shores of Portugal, where he would serve as the guest of honor. Still, he got that old feeling in the pit of his stomach when the plane took off from the runway.

Propped up in a chair by the fortress doors of the winery, the decorated war veteran slumped forward under the weight of medals tugging at both lapels. As the congregation filed by to pay their respects, Pilot Officer Winkie clutched each outstretched hand as if it were his last hold on this world. The Anglican Church promised another.

"Marvelous! Marvelous!" Bilkington Bustle continued to proclaim, too near the pub to break stride and shake hands even with a decorated veteran. However, he did hesitate, if only momentarily when the familiar voice of a lady reached him.

"Bilkington! Yoo-hoo! Remember our dance at the Battle of Britain Ball, years ago?"

The reek of *Estée Lauder* told him it must be Tookie Jack, the only piece of crumpet he had ever wanted but failed to conquer. Their dance took place just after the war ended. He had since chased her to the Algarve to no avail. "You recovered so magnificently from the fall that everyone assumed it was just a daring dance step," she laughed.

"It's the fall from grace from which I've not been able to recover," he winked, drawing closer. "Not so loud, my dear. My wife is near." To be sure, that night on the dance floor many years ago was the closest he had ever come to conquering Tookie Jack. Since then, Tookie married Copper Jack and ran away with him to Portugal.

Mrs Bustle's distance from her husband, on the other hand, resulted from a marriage that fell far short of expectations he'd never wanted fulfilled in the first place. She attracted sympathizers for having to endure Bustle as a husband, earned their scorn for having lost him as a lover and was a rudderless boat without him. "I suppose we could find a seat," he finally surrendered, offering Mrs Bustle a begrudging arm.

He was irritated that he felt responsible for his wife's advanced senility. He was equally irritated that he still fancied Tookie Jack after all these years. He was particularly peeved that the pub closed early and the memorial church service would almost certainly run long. As the congregation finally settled into stiff-backed seats, Bustle swallowed a craving for his usual Sunday morning comforts, the golf green and his wine flask.

All eyes followed Reverend Pat's gaze into the open-beamed rafters of the bodega's high-arched ceiling. A vulgar Adam's apple danced above the reverend's starched white collar. He swallowed hard, searching the heavens for inspiration when he needed it most.

"Friends," he began finally, lowering his head slowly and cupping his hands on the bar, "in our hearts, in our own way, let us pray." Long 'aahs' reverberated in the ceiling above: bowed neck bones were offered in prayer, shriveled neck bones for the most part, with not enough meat collectively to flavor a kettle of soup.

A fly circled overhead before parking itself directly on Reverend Pat's bald pate, providing him with an elusive religious tingle from an unknown source. Pilot Officer Winkie, who sat dutifully in the corner biding his time, had prayed many times at the helm of his fighter plane. Today, without a flashing dashboard of splenetic needles and dials to command his attention, and without a mesmerizing Messerschmitt darting in and out of his gun sight demanding his full concentration, the former pilot snored unabashedly during the sermon from his post by the front door.

Bilkington Bustle had no knack for prayer. He fidgeted in his seat, perspiring heavily. His spindly legs cramped when he crossed them and tingled with sleep when he relaxed them. He tried to ignore his chair, which was squeaking rudely whenever he shifted his weight. His heavy splash of aftershave was even more impossible to ignore.

As the sermon droned on, Tookie Jack enjoyed a good cry. She had come to lament the death of her first husband who died at the Battle of Arnhem. They had been married on leave (perhaps, of their senses) and in such a rush to tie the knot she was still a virgin when her soldier left the wedding ceremony immediately afterward to return to the front. He was killed six weeks later, making her a widow at the age of nineteen. Although she had remarried twice since, Tookie always attended Battle of Britain church services expecting someone to mention also the importance of the Battle of Arnhem. No one ever did.

"Amen," Reverend Pat finally concluded.

"Amen," the congregation echoed.

"... and serve the gin," Bustle pleaded under his breath, only to be disappointed.

"Hymn one hundred and sixty-four." The Reverend's command brought the congregation to its feet, hymnbooks in hand. On cue, vocal chords scratched forth like cracked rubber across a dry windshield.

"Valley-y-y-y ..." Since he didn't know the words, Bustle hummed along with the organ music. Mrs Bustle ad-libbed words here and there. Pilot Officer Winkie snored while Tookie Jack sniffled. Only the usher, Mr Marrow, who imposed his off-key baritone on the congregation, seemed disappointed when the hymn struggled to completion.

After everyone was seated again, Reverend Pat caught stride.

"Friends, why have we gathered here today and in our religious thoughts chosen to dredge up from infamy an act of war? Because war, as with every momentous event on this earth, unfolds at the hands of God. In this case, it was His way of ridding the world of swastikas and the very Devil himself. If not the chosen land, our Britannia was certainly the chosen battleground for good versus evil. We were His soldiers. Our pilots were His angels. So, without further ado, let me introduce to you one of God's chosen, one of the last: Pilot Officer Winkie of the Royal Air Force."

It was Marrow clearing his throat intentionally like a sub machine gun that finally shook Winkie out of a deep slumber. He jumped to his feet suddenly ready to salute. When he finally realized all eyes were on him, he remembered why. He was supposed to speak, to say something memorable on this 'marvelous' occasion. Gradually, he lurched forward toward the aisle and jingled his war medallions on his chest showily, ultimately depreciating whatever face value they once owned. The donation plate Marrow passed around to the eager congregation was full of cash before the guest of honor uttered a single word.

While making his way slowly up the aisle, Winkie reviewed in his mind the story he had perfected over and over in every British pub he frequented, late evenings when he was so full of horse piss and bullshit even the hero of the moment could no longer separate fact from fiction. So it's the only story Winkie told anymore to the house-nurse who dressed him smartly in his military uniform each and every day for the rest of his life. As he steadied himself behind the pulpit bar with Reverend Pat at his side, Winkie suddenly felt right at home as master storyteller.

If only he could moisten his throat, he thought.

"During the war, the military chef served one egg for breakfast to pilots scheduled to fly reconnaissance that day. Everyone knew, when the cook served up two eggs, it was because you had been ordered into battle. On that fateful day in nineteen-forty, I was still a rather junior pilot with only a few reconnaissance flights under my belt. I remember asking the cook for my customary poached egg. Instead, I got two hard-boiled in return and it wasn't until after the battle I discovered it was a bloody cook's mistake, of all things, that sent me on my first real mission. Before I knew it, there I was, saddled into the cockpit of a shiny Spitfire, with a hot throttle thrust between my legs like a Soho hard-on."

Winkie's last unfortunate simile put an abrupt end to his testimony long before he could reach the final punch line. Bar-room burlesque would be allowed to blunder on, if only to give the audience the opportunity to shell the bad performer with over-ripe tomatoes. However, in the House of God, Winkie's script didn't play well. To cut short the laughter, Reverend Pat quickly summoned forth a round of 'God Save the Queen' and motioned frantically for Marrow to usher the bewildered guest of honor out the back door of the church.

With the church services prematurely aborted, Bilkington Bustle discovered the world to be marvelous again. He led a charge of humanity toward the pulpit (now the bar) that left behind a scatter of random hymnbooks. "I wonder where Winkie parked his Spitfire?" someone asked jokingly.

"Sent us the wrong mental patient, I should think," Bustle answered.

A fresh armada of gin and tonics soon lined the counter of the bar from end to end, completing the customary transition from the Sunday service to Sunday slosh. Liz was the diminutive bar tender and doubled as Mrs Reverend Pat. Along with Bustle, Liz could not feign disappointment with the abbreviated church service; it left more time for drinking. As resident bookkeeper of Casa Bodega, Liz would never let on to the Reverend that proceeds from the Sunday slosh far exceeded the donations from his sermons.

Standing on an orange crate balanced on her tiptoes in order to reach the counter and be seen by her customers, always reminded Liz of her former university days has a history lecturer when her students could barely see her above the lip of the podium. She was a short ninety pounds to pity, until she spoke. Her deep throaty voice managed to keep the world in line. "All right, then. Steady as you go mates. Do keep your powder dry. Got enough gin back here to float all of us across the Atlantic Ocean."

Liz abandoned a stuffy, unfulfilling teaching career late in life to become a hairdresser, only to find she simply couldn't suffer the vanity of every woman who walked through the salon door. So, one day she stormed out the door herself, leaving behind her last tormented customer under a hair dryer, soon to bemoan the head of desert tumbleweed staring back at her in the mirror.

Liz's next career as bartender happened strictly by chance. Reverend Pat was away for the evening delivering a church service at one of the missionaries dotting the Algarve coastline. Lonely and bored, Liz stumbled into the bodega one night and proceeded to get sloshed. Somehow, after midnight, she found herself behind the bar serving drinks and did such a smashing good job, the previous owners hired her. "Can't do the job sober, mind you," she admitted to newcomers surprised to see a woman behind the bar. She was so successful that she and Reverend Pat decided to make an offer to buy Casa Bodega, and the rest was history.

Today, as on every Sunday, the congregation descended upon her, pushing and shoving one another good naturedly. The men always arrived at the bar first and passed back drinks to the ladies, who stood off in polite clusters, pounding back more gin and tonics than did the men. Somewhere among the din of the crowd, Tookie Jack could be heard holding court, drink firmly in hand.

"I can't believe it," Tookie complained. "Not a bloody word for the Battle of Arnhem. The whole thing is ludicrous, unjust, and I shall report it to the archbishop straightaway." Mrs Bustle seemed to agree with her. "It's true. We don't ask much of the Reverend, now do we? Just to christen, marry and bury us when the time comes."

"Well, I've done my bit for the Battle of Arnhem and no more," Tookie declared, knocking back her drink in typically manly fashion.

"Look at them," Bustle observed from the bar, where he drooled over the women from a safe distance. "They all want fucking, but there is no one left to do it for them."

"Except you, of course," Liz mocked him. "The only virile Union Jack left in the Algarve."

"Never mind, Lizard, I'm in mourning myself or I would line them all up and satisfy them one by one. Look at these blistered hands," Bustle pleaded, holding up his open palms for inspection to anyone who would listen. "I drove more than a thousand golf balls off the tee yesterday. Just had to get out of the house and express myself."

Reverend Pat gave Liz a knowing smile. "His favorite brother just croaked off," he whispered, "and didn't leave Bustle a single farthing of his vast fortune."

In his rather public mourning, Bustle's soliloquy continued without bounds or discretion. "It grieves me. Really grieves me. How many times did I wire my brother to come down to the Algarve where we could have lived the good life together doing all the things we like best? Going out in the boat and fishing all morning, a round of golf in the afternoon and downing a few kidney flushers at night. And what did he do with his fortune instead? Bought a bloody castle for some young wench – at the far end of the world – only to endure her screwing around behind his back, as he slowly passed away on his death bed. Somehow he still found it in his heart to leave her all of his fortune. And not even a ruddy shilling of gratitude for his blood-kin brother, if you can believe that. Please don't spread the word around, Lizard," he suddenly whispered. "Don't want to discourage some wench eager to court a gentleman with potential, now do I?" A suggestive glance from Frill Pimpton at the end of the bar reminded Bustle he suddenly possessed something equally powerful to offer the ladies, ever since a couple of nights ago.

He recalled how the evening wind snake-charmed a steady rattle against the French door of Frill Pimpton's farm villa, where she crouched deep in the folds of Freddy's overstuffed easy chair, studying her husband's pitiful mug in the fading photograph above the mantel. Flames from the fireplace danced in her bifocals. She fondled an empty gin bottle in her lap for pleasure.

Freddy Pimpton arrived in the Algarve on a fifth of a lung. After his sudden death, Frill Pimpton tried to return to the UK on a fifth of gin. "That's medication where I come from," she explained to the authorities. Of course the customs officer would have none of her shenanigans and sent her back to the Algarve to dry out. Frill detested their farm villa that slumped forlornly on five unfarmed acres outside the village. The villa had been Freddy's bright idea following a brief visit. He decided immediately that the clean Algarve air suited his shriveling lung.

Soon after moving into his new villa, however, Freddy began shitting his bed uncontrollably. Cancer of the bowels was diagnosed. The condition was temporarily arrested after an emergency operation in Lisbon. Yet, when he returned home, a bedpan was kept under his bed as a precaution because Portuguese plumbing was infamous for springing leaks. During Freddy's ongoing fight with cancer, Frill did not remind anyone of Florence Nightingale. She moved herself first to a twin bed next to his bed before evacuating their bedroom all together, complaining of foul odors.

Eventually, it was Freddie's bad bowels and lung that did him in. Fighting a chest cold, his lung proved no match for the wheezing and coughing that ensued. His body kicked up his legs in quick surrender.

Freddy's portrait above the mantel now repulsed Jill. It was a stark reminder of how Freddy's illness, over time, melted away his masculine features. Cold black eyes diminished gradually into sorrowful, unfocused holes in his head. A once angular jaw sank into slack and flabby jowls. Broad, definitive shoulders became slippery slopes. Massively knuckled hands, locked passively over a protruding waistline, measured the rise and fall of each halting breath. Even worse, his prolonged inactivity left Freddy increasingly gutless below the belt. So long did the malaise linger over their relationship, Frill swore on the Bible that Freddy lost his health and virility as far back in time as the hotel suite during their honeymoon. Still, up until his bowel troubles, they slept as man and wife. Frill would lie awake at his side each morning, pretend to read a book and wait for the first signs his heavy body was about to stir. With his first broken snore, she explored the open fly of Freddy's pajama bottoms and made him stiff before the sleep cleared from his eyes and she saw it as no Victorian heresy if she was required to mount Freddy like a horse to get her feminine fill. For his part, Freddy endured Frill's sexual fantasies like a champ. He felt he owed her at least that much. Disabled much of his life, odds are that even a healthy Freddy would have struggled to satisfy Frill's appetite and she seldom let him forget it.

Bilkington Bustle stood outside Frill's farm villa in the darkness, peeking through the curtain-less French doors and making imaginary faces at her through the glass window. After realizing he was only entertaining himself because Frill could not see him in the darkness, he knocked twice, paused, then knocked twice more in the secret code of an otherwise well-publicized affair. "Come in, Bilkington. No one here but us apparitions," Frill replied, a bit peeved to have to remove the gin bottle from between her chubby thighs.

"I'll get us a fresh bottle," Bustle volunteered, moving instinctively toward the living room bar.

"We really don't need it. I'm already pretty far along really and I don't want anything to interfere with your performance," Frill announced when Bustle arrived with the gin. "Prepare the bed," she ordered. "I'll be along shortly." Bustle held his ground and stared eye-to-eye at the photo of Freddy Pimpton above the fireplace.

"I say. Don't you find this picture of your former husband intolerably morose?"

"Go make the bed," she insisted. "Or have you forgotten the way?"

"I should forget the way to my favorite pub first," Bustle said, before taking a bow and then disappearing down a long, dark hallway.

As soon as he had gone, Frill lit a candle beneath Freddy's portrait and opened the lid to a small music box perched on the mantel alongside the photo. She removed her wedding ring from the music box and placed it on her finger, while Mendelsohn's wedding march tinkled ceremoniously where it had left off the last time. However, this time, Bustle lingered in the shadows of the hallway just outside the living room, studying the strange kneeling figure before the homemade altar, and trying his best not to laugh.

"Freddy," she hesitated, as if one must give the dead time to rise. "As you can see, I come to you tonight still your lawful wedded wife, with a request. Wherever you are, your lonely and faithful wife would like your permission to go to bed with another man."

Bustle tried to escape unnoticed, only it was too late. He exploded into high-pitched giggles before he could reach the bedroom.

"Ha-ha-ha-ha-ha! Ha-ha-ha-ha-ha! PERMISSION? Since when?" Bustle blurted out incredulously. When he finally reached the bedroom, he fell on the bed and buried his face in a pillow, trying to muffle his laughter long after the damage was done.

Even in her fury and embarrassment, Frill methodically returned the ring to the music box, closed the lid and blew out the candle before suddenly charging into the bedroom in an absolute rage. She collapsed on Bustle's body, punishing him with blows. "You bastard!" she gasped, digging her feisty little fists into his backside. "You sacrilegious son-of-a-bitch! You iconoclastic scoundrel! You pretentious pimp! You effeminate con-man!"

Bustle finally came up for air, convulsing with laughter and shielding his face with a pillow as best he could. He finally managed to free himself and stood by the bedside undressing, rather anti-climatically, he thought. His billowy briefs and long argyle socks met near his knees. He appeared like an innocent schoolboy until moonlight shined through the bedroom window, highlighting his manhood, already at half-mast and rising up quickly through the fly of his underwear.

"Well, bloody hell," was all Bustle could manage to say as Frill kissed the tip of his organ until it bled milk.

Brown-skinned senoritas pushed dining room chairs and tables together, painting the bodega into a worldlier version of the Last Supper (more like a Hogarth on closer inspection). The crowd at the bar smelled the stray aromas from the kitchen beginning to stream into the open dining area. As the crowd started to migrate from the bar to the dining room, Bustle and Liz continued to keep everyone entertained with their animated back-chat.

"If not a good husband, at least I could make someone a good golf partner," Bustle boasted.

"Caddy, you mean. I hear arthritis has played havoc with your tee shot," Liz teased.

"Still a bloody irreproachable putter," Bustle insisted.

Liz couldn't resist. "Play croquet with the women then." Bustle got distracted suddenly and ignored the barb.

"Speaking of women, look at this delectable morsel. Pour me a glass of *vino tinto*, senorita, if you will be so kind."

"Si, senor." The Portuguese waitress managed to hold Bustle spellbound by her every move. As she left their table behind, a gust of afternoon breeze slipped through the fortress doors of the bodega and rustled her gala, ankle-length gown pulled tight against her narrow waist. Her child-like feet seemed to bounce playfully along the earthen floor. Straight jet-black hair fell against her naked shoulders. Bustle imagined the senorita perspiring lightly somewhere beneath her dress.

"Keep your eyes on your plate, Bustle. Frill would not be flattered if you called tonight with some undesirable filth between your legs," Liz warned.

"Not that one, Lizard. They don't come any cleaner than her. I'd love to get her in the kitchen." Unfortunately for Bustle, the pitcher of wine was delivered by a waiter—not the young senorita Bustle so admired. However, he was sandwiched delightfully between Liz and Virgo, so at least he had Virgo nearby to keep him titillated.

"It's on me, Bustle," Virgo said, pouring generously from the carafe of wine. "My deepest condolences, of course, for the loss of your brother and, at the same time congratulations to you for wooing Frill Pimpton. She cancelled her appointment with me recently. Looks like I may have lost my best customer, thanks to you."

"I'm sure I don't see the connection, my dear," Bustle objected, although he had heard the same rumors about Virgo along with everyone else on the Algarve. Virgo was the local masseuse and star gazer. She worked out of an upstairs bedroom of the bodega. The services she provided the community were as mysterious as her loyal clientele of women. They never admitted to visiting Virgo. Neither would their husbands, if their husbands were unlucky enough to find out about it. What really puzzled Bustle was what a reasonably young, good-looking woman like her did for adventure among this colony of

British geriatrics. He finally decided to give Virgo every opportunity to clear the air about her occupation. "What are you doing for our women that we can't?" Bustle asked abruptly.

"Haven't seen Mrs Bustle just yet, so don't be so defensive, Bustle," she said, trying to reassure him. "But since you asked, I provide relaxation, confidence, intangibles, really. Can't get into it now, love, I'm off upstairs to have a bath. Here is my card. Arrange an appointment sometime."

As Virgo mounted the stairway of the bodega, Liz answered him before Bustle could even ask the question. "She pays the rent on time and that's all I care to know."

Bustle allowed his mind to wander with Virgo up the stairway to her room. In his imagination, he entered Virgo's room without knocking. Hot steam oozed from the bathroom door left slightly ajar. A black bra and nylons draped over the back of a chair. Tea steeped in a pot on a table littered with business cards. Like the card she gave him, *'By Appointment Only'*: embossed words that lit up in the dark like teeth. The only light among the shadows came from a dingy lampshade in the corner, where a tumble of books on the floor leaned shelf-less against a wall: astrology, massage, herbs. A portable training table rested beneath a darkly shuttered window. Bustle imagined removing his shoes and stretching out on the portable leather table, curious to see what might happen next. He realized he had had a lot to drink. The gas heater hummed in the corner and made him drowsy. He closed his eyes, imagining the Portuguese waitress dressed only in dancing tights with frictionless thighs. He awoke with his foot resting in warm water facing his competitor. Without her makeup on, her face was more wrinkled than he remembered. 'Can always put a sack over their head' was the philosophy he followed in his own love life.

"You fell asleep," she whispered. With a Portuguese ballerina, he thought to himself. "Feet are sensitive," she acknowledged. Portuguese feet once spat grape juice between their toes on the very floors of the bodega, he remembered. "Nerve center reaches every part of your body," she said, fondling his toes and smiling up at the slight bulge beginning to swell in his fly, begging freedom.

"You ought to keep the door locked at moments like this," he recommended: *attractive enough to get raped with her black bra showing prominently through her white blouse, he thought.*

"I knew you were coming," she responded, running her thumb aggressively across the sole of his foot. *Coming? Not yet. If you will just be patient, he thought.* "I'm usually not this forward, mind you." She rested his foot in the pan of warm water and read him a passage from a dog-eared book. "As a Sagittarius, you are ruled by Jupiter. Your sign rules everything large." *Like his groin growing unruly.* "You are highly idealistic." *Imagine the Portuguese waitress sliding into a see-through night gown praying to the Virgin Mary.*

"Your faith sorely tested." *Years of impotence until his coming-out party with Frill Pimpton.* "Until now, too many things out of your hands." *Couldn't jerk off because his privates would fall off, they told him as a kid.* "You will attract an affectionate, more stable love." *No doubt, his masseuse smiling broadly as he burst at the belt, recalling from memory her ass as she walked up the stairs, like a hemisphere to hold in each hand to part at the equator.*

After massaging his other foot, Virgo ran her hand up his pant leg, sparking interest in tendrils of body hair high up on his thigh. She rested her breasts against his shins.

"How much do I owe you for the massage," Bustle finally asked, propping himself up on one elbow and reaching for his wallet, while staring over the biggest hard-on he had ever mustered.

"Privileged customers are allowed to barter for my services," she smiled.

Still in the bodega dining room, Bustle woke up too soon from his erotic fantasy without ever getting to savor the vulgar joy in Virgo's face. Because the vivid images he conjured up were nothing more than a marvelous dream of a delusional old man.

2

To Win the War with Errol Flynn

Most of the congregation had headed home for late afternoon tea by the time Copper Jack strode into the bodega looking for his wife, Tookie.

"Copper Jack!" exclaimed Reverend Pat from the bar. "I don't recall seeing you with Tookie at the church services this morning."

"How's it with you, Reverend? Liz? Everything under control?" Copper asked, taking a bar stool and offering his outstretched hand. "I see the church is still prospering," he said, pointing to the Reverend's unfortunate expanding paunch. The Reverend was quick to return the barb.

"And what are you passing yourself off as today, Copper, the local agnostic?"

"An agnostic is nothing more than an atheist who's afraid to admit it, Reverend. That's my wife, Tookie. She comes to your service once a year for a good cry, and if that happens, then it's a jolly good sermon. So congratulations for that. As for me, I'm a devout atheist. Your wife, Liz, can attest to that. You'll only see me at the bar on Sunday."

"I'm not writing you off that easily, Copper Jack. You're a good man in your heart. A Christian, in fact, if I squinted my eyes hard enough and don't look too carefully. So overcome with pride that you can't even get down on your knees with the rest of us."

Copper took a deep breath before answering. "Maybe that's because during the war I saw many a good soldier killed when a mate at his side hit his knees to pray when he should have been firing his weapon."

Liz interjected, trying to find a common ground between two men she loved. "I just think Patrick figured you might show up for the memorial service." She poured Copper a brandy and lit him a cigarette. "We've all heard the stories, Copper Jack. No use pretending you were anything but a war hero, and we are all grateful."

Copper winced a bit, knocked back his brandy and took a long drag from his cigarette. He realized Tookie had been talking too much again. "Liz, I remember like yesterday shooting down German war planes. Those images never leave you. I also remember how little time I had to think about it, simply had to kill them before they killed me, just a matter of survival. Only when we come together in overblown ceremonies like today do we actually glorify killing when we should be condemning it."

Reverend Pat was still smarting more from Pilot Officer Winkie's unfortunate performance than he was from Copper's criticism, which he heard often enough. "Afraid there wasn't much glory today after all, Copper Jack."

"So why am I suddenly doing all the preaching? You are the man of words. I only came here to retrieve Tookie before she embarrassed herself."

"Already has," Liz confessed, rolling her eyes and shaking her head. The Reverend clarified his wife's show of disgust.

"It appears, Copper, she left earlier today in the arms of Bilkington Bustle." Liz quickly poured Copper another brandy to deaden the pain of bad news.

As a young lad, Copper Jack would speak only when spoken to, at dinner table conversations with his family, where adults complained about the problems of the 1920s: poverty, unemployment and a horrific prime minister, only to face the same problems at dinner the next evening. Year after year nothing seemed to change. After he cleaned his plate each night, Copper would gnash his teeth privately, waiting for the adults at the table to finish their meals so he could be excused properly from the dinner table. In this unwilling process, Copper heard over and over again about the plight of the working man: "How to eat?" was the unyielding quandary of the times. At the Jack's dinner table, you filled your hungry tummy by listening.

By the time Copper Jack was old enough to express his own opinions at the dinner table, he dreamed of sitting in Parliament and actually sorting out the problems of the common man. He would be a political rebel. That is, until his dream was rudely interrupted by the sudden outbreak of World War II. Without question, his ambitions for Parliament would have to wait. Robin Hood would have to cool his heels alone in Sherwood Forest.

There was no hesitation on Copper's part. At the age of 18, he was off to win the war like the American actor, Errol Flynn, whose image on the big screen loomed larger than life itself. In Copper's mind, it was only a matter of how long Hitler could afford sending Messerschmitts into the teeth of his artillery gun. Copper stood his ground proudly on the deck of the ship, chomping down on rubber ear-inserts he held in his mouth to keep his teeth from rattling, while pummeling the heavens with well-aimed ammunition. In the process of battle, he lost a set of teeth chewing through the inserts, and with the inserts in his mouth instead of his ears, he also lost much of his hearing. Yet his aim was good and Jerry pilots quickly identified his ship's gun as the canon barrel that glowed the most during battle. The nickname 'Copper' was his battery mates' acknowledgement of the intense, red-hot color his gun took on during aerial attacks.

Even though Dunkirk turned out to be a miraculous military retreat that saved the lives of thousands of soldiers, Errol Flynn's script tarnished a bit. Privately, British soldiers cursed the 'frogs' inability to defend their own country and they must have looked warily over their own shoulders in retreat, wondering how long it would be before their own homeland would come under assault from the greatest war machine in history.

When Hitler's bombers finally came calling in wave after wave of firepower, Copper and his fellow Englishmen could only squirm uncomfortably in the shadows cast by German squadrons over the streets of London. His ship, along with most of the British navy, was in dry dock without enough ammunition or the ability to fight back. And the German bombers were too far out of the range of Copper Jack's spit. So, restless for any kind of action, Copper finally volunteered to scurry along London rooftops alongside fifty, sixty and seventy-year-old veterans of the First War. As fire watchmen, they patrolled London rooftops armed with the only weapons they had, broomsticks and axe handles. Their mission was to extinguish the flames from German incendiary baskets dropped as targets to assist the accuracy of German bomber raids to follow.

Britain's only defense at the time came out of necessity when the Royal Air Force was suddenly called into action. As ill-prepared as they may have been in the beginning, in the end they became a lethal fighting machine. So famous were their exploits, in the years following the war, every Englishman in every pub gathering across the country would claim to have flown a Spitfire in the Battle of Britain. Winston Churchill said it best: "Never in the field of human conflict was so much owed by so many to so few." Decals suddenly became popular on warplanes, Hollywood launched a new movie script and Copper Jack, on the ground, chewed through his last pair of ear inserts in anonymity, while real history was being made in the skies, knowing he was one of the many who owed so much.

However, when the date approached to join the Allied invasion at Normandy, Copper was a Navy artillery commander and this time he had all the ammunition he needed, thanks to the Lease-Lend agreement negotiated with their Allies. Copper's job was to train artillery gunners, an occupation where teamwork was especially vital, because gunners on every ship depended on one another. That is why Copper refused to accept Private Lunt into his unit for the Normandy invasion. Lunt admitted to getting cold feet as soon as the shooting started. Copper knew all too well that even a mediocre German pilot would take full advantage of any gun that goes silent during battle. Copper's military unit would be swimming the English Channel should Lunt freeze up in action.

As a result, Copper sent Lunt to the medic with the private's full confession. The medic returned Lunt to his post with a simple explanation: if every soldier's fear earned him a reassignment to peel potatoes below the deck, there would soon be no one left to fight. Copper bristled at the fact that a quack could overrule an artillery commander, so he came up with another plan for Private Lunt.

"Now, all you have to do," he told Lunt when they arrived in dry dock, "is walk down the street, pick out the first British sergeant you see, and punch him in the mug. I'll arrest you and throw you in the brig. I'll get my new gunner after all and in the process you'll have saved your own neck."

Lunt dwarfed Copper Jack as they walked side-by-side down the streets of Portsmouth and cruel fate placed Copper's old friend, Jimmy Toban, in Lunt's direct path. No taller than Copper Jack, Toban tipped the scales at 150 pounds soaking wet. Copper knew him to be feisty and high-spirited, and sure enough, Toban swaggered forward to greet Copper with a smile. Lunt recognized the newly-earned sergeant stripes before Copper did and he saluted, stepped forward and lifted the sergeant from the ground with a strong right-hand uppercut that deposited Toban in a heap on the side of the street. He lay motionless on the ground, cradling his jaw between his palms, while Lunt admired his own clenched fist immodestly. Copper rushed Lunt to the brig and Toban to the dentist.

After the dentist performed his magic and salvaged most of Toban's teeth, Copper treated Toban to a beer, which he had to suck through puffy lips with a straw. Copper couldn't resist needling his best friend. "Got to keep that left guard up. Never lead with your stripes, sergeant."

Sergeant Toban had the last laugh when Lunt was returned to his post again as a ship gunner in Copper's outfit. Apparently Lunt's knockout victory over Sergeant Toban awakened the savage within him. Wanting no part in another scheme to avoid conflict, Lunt blew the whistle on Copper.

Copper was put up for court martial, which suited him more than leading recruits like Lunt into battle but instead of a court martial, his otherwise stellar military record earned him a second chance: a post in the Air Force as turret gunner on a British bomber brigade, a position infamous to all military personnel as a one-way ticket to Cloud Nine.

After a couple of weeks dodging Messerschmitts under the glass bubble, Copper would have preferred his chances alongside Lunt, kneeling and praying on the beaches of Normandy. When his transfer request was denied by the Royal Air Force, he transferred himself the next time his feet touched ground by walking across the street and joining the Army. The Air Force is still looking for him.

The Army did not greet Copper with open arms. Perhaps he swaggered too much in his civvies. When the attendant threw him a uniform twice his size, Copper threw it back across the counter as an insult. When the attendant followed up by suggesting that Copper *"couldn't fill a real man's uniform,"* Copper threw himself across the counter.

The Army was so impressed by Copper's hand-to-hand combat technique that he wound up hitting the beaches of Normandy after all, this time as a front-line ground hog. He provided ground cover on the beaches for the advancement, playing the tedious infantry war game of dig in and hold, dig in and hold, while the real action leapfrogged, beyond him and the infantry, to entirely new battle fronts. After his retreat from Dunkirk, Copper's return to French soil was a script still not juicy enough for Errol Flynn.

Following the Allied force's success at Normandy, thousands of healthy British military men stretched out on miles of open ocean beaches, sunning themselves under clear skies, waiting for the paperwork to be processed, which would return them home to civilian life. With time on their hands, they had nothing to do but celebrate. They had just fought and won a war. The enemy now was boredom.

Copper happened to be stationed in Belgium where money, sunshine and venereal disease were plentiful. Since they could not take Belgian currency back to England with them when their discharge came through, each soldier took his turn treating the entire barracks to a party. Champagne flowed for months during the time it took to get all the men back safely across the Channel. With all the alcohol they consumed, they could have floated across the ocean without boats.

When Copper finally returned home after the war, he discovered he was the only member of his village football team to survive military service. In six years of distinguished duty for three branches of the military, he had crossed the English Channel to Dunkirk and Normandy, and been fished out of the sea on more occasions than he could remember. Nevertheless, he refused to apply for any of the war medals for which he had been recommended. He had no desire to stand head and shoulders above military mates who had died at his side, making him a hero.

Copper also returned home to the responsibility of supporting his war-time bride, dashing his dreams forever of becoming a Member of Parliament. Needing to earn money, Copper buried his regrets in a few acres of his family's fertile land in Kent, and settled down to become a successful dirt farmer like his father.

If his marriage soon became a disappointment, farming became a tragedy. In time Copper managed to build up a prosperous business as a major pork supplier for nearby villages but just when his farm was beginning to turn a profit, swine flu hit England in epidemic proportions. The government slaughtered Copper's entire supply of livestock as a precaution. At this low point in his life Copper chanced to meet Tookie.   As he admitted many times in later years, "She turned my life around."

3

Until Death Do Us Part

The familiar silhouette hunched beneath the yellow light of a lampshade. The portable radio forever at his side was tuned to a BBC overseas news broadcast that alternately swelled in volume and stuttered in faint whisper. The embrace of his armchair and the usual brandy and cigarette before dawn served to steady his nerves against the always-somber news events from abroad, the 'stupidities of man', he called them.

After the broadcast ended, he snuffed his butt in a tray erupting with ashes. He unrolled clean socks, noticed with annoyance they were not a matching pair, and stuffed them in his pocket until daylight.

They say that when Copper Jack begins to wear socks beneath his cotton slippers, winter has descended upon the Algarve. A sometimes-mist and rare frost stretch into long nights, chilling orange-tiled village roofs and smoldering, snoring embers. Surf rocks a distant shore, closer by ear than foot, where lonely Portuguese fishing boats battle the Atlantic sea by lantern.

A fortune teller could read, by morning shadow, the recurring oddity etched in Copper's leathery palm. He had lived a lifetime in winter: off to war; a first marriage; sudden poverty; his first divorce; and now his wife, Tookie, leaving the church service yesterday with Bilkington Bustle. Fate followed even the unbelieving and could forgive Copper another brandy and smoke on this first dawn of another ominous winter season.

Copper cherished these early morning vigils. Most of his day was cluttered with former English colonialists, friends and foes, whom he humored. To all he offered a curious ear. At one time or another everyone cuddled up alongside his armchair, loosened their tongues drinking his liquor, voluntarily parading skeletons from their private lives to Copper's very own doorstep. He permitted their trespass upon his privacy because early on in his retirement he decided that loneliness is the most perplexing disease known to man. His fee then was to suffer their modest company, such as it was; in consequence, he recreated a version of Piccadilly Circus in his very own living room.

Copper turned off the wireless once the morning news cycle started to repeat itself, and left the comfort of his armchair in favor of a brisk stroll in the garden outside. Standing alone and gazing into the bright sunrise, he seemed taller than he was, a Napoleonic five-and-a-half feet. His still handsome face was cut in jagged edges like a broken beer bottle, the kind of rugged features that played havoc with a razor blade but stood out in a crowd: cold cheekbones, talon nose, and anvil jaw – facial bones that jutted forward distinctly. The hair flared outward from bushy eyebrows, winged and pointy-edged, and silver tufts of curl bristled on his head like wire in the wind. Few wrinkles lined the face as the skin was still drawn tight at the chin. It was a memorable face worth minting on coins and chiseling into mountainsides.

In the distance, a dog barked and a farmer shouted in Portuguese, herding the sheep together, side-by-side, as they did every morning. "Copper Jack! What is all the barking about?" Tookie bellowed from the back porch with all the coarseness of a Billingsgate fishwife.

"Just a farmer and his dog trying to do their daily job – and from the sour tone of your voice this morning you might try getting out on the other side of the bed before addressing me today," he challenged her. His tart response was greeted by a woman's slipper sailing over his head, just missing the mark, which irritated Tookie even more.

"And you might have your tongue loose from your cheek by then, Copper Jack!" she shouted, turning her six-foot frame around and heading defiantly back to the bedroom, saving formal rebuttal for a more civilized hour of day.

In frustration, Copper hurled his pair of unmatched socks in her general direction. "If you've nothing better to do, walk through the village, then, and frighten all the children," he shouted long after she deserted him. The hoot of a nearby hoopoe bird mocked this man's brave return to his castle.

Their original love for one another was severely tested during a long, ten-year courtship that Tookie finally managed to whittle to nine. They met in a hospital in Kent where Tookie was bedridden with kidney stones and Copper worked as a part-time ambulance driver. Copper took one glance at her in the recovery room and predicted privately to himself, "I'm going to screw that within a fortnight," even though Tookie always insists she managed to hold him off for several months whenever she is telling the story. "You've got to be joking," Copper said, standing by his testimony, "would not have waited that long for any woman. In the Army, I could have had better than you for a pack of cigarettes."

"And what were you, pray tell, an ambulance driver who also smelled of pigs."

At least for Copper, it had been a case of lust at first sight. Copper answered an emergency call while on duty, arriving at Tookie's street address to find her unconscious in the living room. Behind the wheel of the ambulance, he sent innocent bicyclists careening into bushes along the narrow back roads rushing her to the hospital.

A few days later, Copper passed the recovery room and saw Tookie, weak and feeble, wave off her nurse who approached with a wheel chair. She literally willed herself to the ladies room under her own power. From that day on, Copper went out of his way to visit the recovery room to remind Tookie she had a standing dinner invitation as soon as she recovered. "I'm married with four children, I am, and don't conduct my life that way, thank you very much," was Tookie's steadfast rejection, which she repeated every time Copper came calling.

Once she found out from the nurse that Copper, too, was married, her decision was final, except someone forgot to inform her ambulance driver. She agonized for months in the hospital under the effects of a strict water diet. The loss of weight sapped her strength, but at least the kidney stones finally shifted enough and she no longer clawed away at her own flesh in absolute pain. Mercifully, when the day finally came for her release from the hospital, Tookie preferred Copper's fresh anemone blossoms over the many other bouquets adorning her hospital room. The calling card was signed simply, "His Majesty." Against her doctor's orders and her own sense of morality, she accepted Copper's dinner invitation for later in the week.

As with most couples, their courtship was the romance. Every species on earth saves its best coat for courting. Tookie decided to celebrate the special occasion by slipping into a sleek-fitting blue suit trimmed in mink to highlight her new, hard-won slimness. Leading up to her dinner date with Copper Jack, she spent every waking hour of the day modeling her new suit in front of the mirror. When Saturday finally arrived, she confessed in her diary that she was madly in love and very thankful her blue suit 'fitted' the occasion.

Like a good ambulance driver, Copper arrived punctually, rapping on Tookie's brass door-knocker with a sense of urgency. After opening the front door, Tookie clung to the doorknob for several moments to help steady her shaky legs. They were observing one another for the first time wearing clothing other than hospital garb, and they both liked what they saw. Overcome with emotion, they embraced without needing any words to comfort them. With sentiment duly observed, Copper decided it was time to test Tookie's timbre. Just how strong a person was she really he wondered? He announced suddenly he had come to take her fishing, suggesting she could cook over a campfire, for their dinner, whatever they caught.

Tookie stepped back from Copper with an incredulous look on her face, trying desperately to measure his seriousness. He was immaculately dressed in a handsome suit and tie, his face lit up in an irrepressibly schoolboy grin, so Tookie assured herself Copper must be joking. Even after they got in the car and drove directly to a nearby lake outside the village, Tookie still couldn't believe Copper was serious about going through with this. Once he got out of the car and retrieved his fishing tackle and poles from the boot of his car, Tookie dug in her high heels. She refused to get out of the car even after he opened her door like a true gentleman. As Copper sat the butt of his corduroy trousers carefully on a nearby tree stump, casting his fishing line into the lake, Tookie scowled back at him through the car windshield.

Under normal circumstances, in her fury, Tookie would have thought nothing about driving Copper's car into the lake in retaliation. Instead, she checked her emotions, deciding to beat Copper at his own game. She marched dutifully down the embankment of the lake, picked up the extra fishing pole and cast her line as if she knew what she was doing. She fished with enthusiasm and stubbornly refused to speak or look in Copper's direction. She reeled in frequently with imagined tugs at her line, only they were all false alarms because she had forgotten to bait her hook in the first place. Copper fought back smiles as he studied her from the corner of his eye. She cut a fine figure in her mink fishing outfit, he decided. He was particularly attracted by the way her outfit gathered well above the knees when she found a tree stump of her own liking to sit on.

As the afternoon light began to fade, leaving the two stubborn fishermen to sit in gray evening shadows until the other one cried uncle, it was Copper who finally decided Tookie had more than proven her mettle and called the game off. He suggested they seek out a nice restaurant since they had both failed to catch their dinner. Even in reconciliation, Copper couldn't pass up the opportunity to needle Tookie with stories about 'the one that got away'. "Had you remembered to bait your hook, the big fella teasing your fishing line would have satisfied our appetites quite nicely, I should think." In the gathering darkness, Tookie finally surrendered a reluctant smile of her own.

In the aftermath of their aborted fishing expedition, Tookie and Copper laughed, danced and drank the night away. In between, they ate ravenously as Tookie stretched her shrunken stomach with quantities of spicy pork well beyond the imposed limits of her prescribed hospital diet. The mink trim around her collar seemed to purr contentedly well into the late hours. It was not until she was alone in bed later that night when her dinner binge resulted in a severe attack of stomach cramps. "He tried to kill me! Copper tried to kill me!" she exaggerated. "The bloody lout tried to poison me!" she shrieked into the night hysterically, releasing all of her stored up venom from the fishing fiasco and prompting her husband, Raymond, to make a rare appearance in her bedroom.

"Whoever he is, he owes me no favors," Raymond announced sullenly and left the room as quickly as he arrived. A flower vase crashed against the closed door behind him.

Somehow she managed to survive the night and Copper didn't fare well in her diary entry the next morning. Yet the next time Copper came calling, all was forgiven except for Tookie's waistline, which was expanding as rapidly as her love for Copper. All Copper said to her by way of proposing their first illicit weekend together was: "Pack your bag. You are spending the weekend with me," and without a moment's hesitation, Tookie obediently tossed her suitcase into the backseat of his Hillman.

As they drove along, the road bounded joyously through the lush green English countryside. When the Hillman suddenly slowed to a crawl with the approach of a sterling blue lake on their left, then came to a complete stop near a lonely camper's tent carefully pitched among a clearing of trees, Tookie began to have her doubts. "Well, here we are then," Copper announced.

Tookie was aghast. Understandably, the lurid image of a mother of four groveling on the ground all weekend in a camping tent didn't sit well with her. Fortunately for her, before she could raise any objections, a fisherman and his wife stepped outside of their tent, just as Copper stepped on the gas and the Hillman continued merrily on down the road. He had fooled her again. Realizing she had once again been victimized by Copper's practical joke, Tookie leaned against the dashboard of the Hillman and burst into laughter. Copper cackled out loud as well. Both of them were in rare form when they finally reached their destination at Thatcher's Inn later that evening.

The old inn stood proudly in the once desolate Lower Downs in the days before land developers gobbled up all the available farmlands. A horse stable still leaned precariously against the side of the inn from a day when the only travelers came by coach. Old country pub flavor greeted visitors indoors: a roaring inglenook fireplace, the warm light of kerosene, sawdust on the floor at their feet. A flurry of darts and conversation filled the air. Copper scribbled the name 'the Jacks' onto the register without blinking at the proprietor of the Inn, and he and Tookie followed a wizened little old fellow, overdressed in tails, up a cozy stairway to the guest rooms. Their room was not much larger than the double bed it housed and since it was considered the 'daughter's room' in this old converted Victorian cottage, its occupants had no alternative except to pass through the 'parents' room' to visit the bathroom or, more to the point, to escape from the house after hours, without the parents' permission. The attendant chuckled when informing them that the adjoining 'parents 'room' just happened to be reserved for a honeymoon couple who would arrive shortly.

After dinner in the dining room downstairs, Tookie retired immediately to their bedroom to enjoy more intimate matters. Because the room was small, she undressed behind the closet door for privacy, while Copper bounced playfully and nakedly on the bed, testing the squeaky bedsprings. Tookie heard all the activity coming from their bed, poked her head around the closet door and whispered into the darkness: "You seem to be doing quite well without me."

Tookie was privately pleased with her body. She had always been a big-boned, long-legged beauty. Her breasts overflowed immodestly through the unlaced bodice. Her thighs pinched gently between the frilled panty legs, but beauty alone was not enough. When Tookie heard the newlyweds enter the adjoining bedroom next door and lock the door behind them, Tookie's personal pride took over.

"O-o-o-o-o-ah-h-h-h-h. Yes, that's it! Oh, deeper!" Tookie groaned, emerging finally from behind the closet door. Copper sprang up like a startled window shade. "O-O-O-O-O-H! Ah-H-H-H-H! More! More! Oh, Copper, YES!"

Copper looked at Tookie in wonderment. "You seem to be doing fine without my help," he retaliated.

"Just don't want the newlyweds next door to feel they're disturbing us," she whispered, pointing to the door they shared between the two adjoining rooms. "Copper?"

"What now?" he asked, not really looking forward to the answer.

"I need to visit the loo," she admitted, which, in this floor plan they both knew, would require a stroll through the newlywed's bedroom in order to reach the bathroom at the end of the hall. Copper was beside himself.

"You've got to be joking!" Her silence assured him she wasn't. "Can't it wait until morning?" he asked.

"Not unless you're up to changing bedpans."

"Well, are you going to knock on the door and upset the honeymooner's momentum? Or do you plan to streak nimbly, passing them in the dark disguised as a 140-pound ocean breeze?"

Tookie got to her feet and took matters into her own hands. She rested her ear against the adjoining door listening intently, while Copper lit a candle and studied the length and beauty of her legs from the shadows across the room. He admired a good pair of legs above all else.

"A bloody burlesque show," he predicted, sitting cross-legged in the middle of the mattress with the bed sheet modestly covering the aroused growth of his privates.

Tookie knocked on the door lightly without getting any response. "Hello. Hello. Is it all right to come in?" Copper choked back laughter. "The newlyweds next door are probably petrified you're trying to organize an orgy."

"They must already be asleep," Tookie determined, blowing out her candle just as she unlocked the door between the two rooms. She was just inside the honeymooners' room when she stumbled in the dark and lurched forward onto the middle of their bed. She landed squarely upon a pair of half-clothed lovers, embracing each other more out of fear than passion.

Tookie and Copper did little to hide their feelings for one another during the courtship. Everyone in the small Kent village knew about the affair. Yet it was important to Tookie to keep face and endure her marriage another ten years until the last of her kids were grown. So, to her four children who saw him often, Copper became known as 'Uncle'. In the meantime, the marriages they both endured were as different as their personalities.

Copper brought his always-stoic nature to a rather innocuous wartime marriage arranged by his mother. After the war ended when the real work of marriage began, Copper decided it did not suit him. With little fanfare, his wife agreed to a divorce whenever he wished. There was so little bitterness between them that Copper's match-maker mother could not question their decision.

Tookie, on the other hand, was emotional and fought Raymond repeatedly in pan-flying, pack-my-bag sequences that kept the neighbors flinching. Tookie was a brawler by nature and kept Raymond constantly on the defensive. Late in their marriage he finally admitted his tendency toward homosexuality, conveniently blaming Tookie for what he perceived as his own inadequacies. Tookie sobbed, threw things and maintained a personal diary of fast-paced narrative.

Finally, after enduring nine years of what was supposed to be a ten-year courtship, Tookie simply couldn't take it anymore. She appeared on Copper's doorstep one day unannounced, bags in hand and moved into Copper's personal caravan parked alongside the cottage he still shared with his wife. It seems Tookie had thrown a slice of melon at the back page of Raymond's London Times, which he always held up to his face to hide behind whenever they had breakfast together.

"What's with you, woman? Are you possessed?" Raymond asked.

"Absolutely! And I'm going to marry my exorcist!"

While Tookie and Copper waited for their divorces to become final, the local minister paid the newly-engaged couple an obligatory call. He dutifully reminded them divorce was against the wishes of the church.

"Reverend, as you know, we don't have much use for the church, so we're not looking for your blessings," Copper reminded him. "Besides, Tookie and I are perfectly matched, like bookends. Tookie is religious so she happens to be my foot in the door of the pearly gates if it turns out there is a god in heaven. And I'm her shoulder to lean on in the real world because I know there isn't one."

Tookie returned to bed, feeling agitated with Copper as she often did these days, eager to close her eyes and pretend this unfortunate start to the day never happened. Likewise, Copper eased back into the comfort of his armchair: sorry he'd ever left it in the first place. He decided to celebrate this first Algarve winter morning with yet another glass of brandy – "So she doesn't drive me crackers," he reminded himself with a sigh.

In spite of Tookie's vocal presence and the constant circle of humanity he allowed to clutter his retirement days, Copper was actually a hermit by nature and had always found Copper Jack interesting enough. For example, he had invested countless morning hours alone, just like this one, contemplating a process for converting garlic into an odorless medication for people suffering from arthritis.

During seven years of solitary dawns, he managed to concoct a system of beating the bookies at the racetrack, "beating them just often enough to pay the rent," he would say, "because if you become too greedy they will find you out and beat you into submission." In these same waking hours he sketched mechanical drawings for a new rotary engine that could revolutionize the automotive industry. Someone beat him to the market with what appeared to be his original idea, and made a fortune that could have been his, if only he had bothered to apply for a patent.

So, in Copper's mind, most of man's genius occurred alone, under poor lighting, on an empty stomach, with only a heartbeat hum in his ears; the time before daylight when the woman breathing easily just down the hallway is his first and only love and time does not change her; the moment in life when he is everything he ever wanted to become and there is not enough daylight in the mirror to reflect otherwise.

It was just this innocent hour of day last winter when Copper woke up early from a sleepless night to catch up on some reading in his favorite armchair. The book spine was barely cracked to the open page, the eyes focused, when a click in his brain left a sentence unfinished and all of the pages blank. Copper cried out, "Tookie, this is no time of day to be playing with the lights." If Tookie rolled over in her sleep, it was the only sign of life in the house. Once Copper realized he also could not see the luminous face of his wristwatch, he waited silently in darkness for daylight that never returned. Tookie found him later that morning still hugging his armchair for dear life.

Specialists were hesitant to diagnose and just as reluctant to promise the return of Copper's eyesight. Strokes were an improbable lot. Even Copper's longtime friend back in the UK, the family doctor in Kent, said there was nothing he could do except monitor Copper's situation and hope his vision would return. At first, Copper dealt with his setback in his own private corner of the world. He stayed in London near his doctor and sent Tookie back to Portugal without him. After a period of time passed and it became obvious Copper's blindness might be more than a temporary affliction, the prescription altered. His doctor feared further separation from Tookie would only delay the difficult adjustment Copper and she would have to make together. So his doctor finally persuaded Copper to rejoin Tookie in Portugal and get on with his life again.

Copper returned and spent the first week home enduring Tookie's pity while she suffered through his prolonged silences. After a week of groping in blindness, Copper matter-of-factly decided to blow his brains out. In the meantime, the first hint of springtime offered a therapy of its own. Almond and mimosa trees blossomed and coastal breezes played in the wheat fields. As Copper returned to semi-normal life, busying himself once again with the personal problems of his many house-guests, he allowed himself fewer hours to meditate on his own plight.

Gradually, partial eyesight returned, from shadows and mysterious shapes, to about half the field of his normal vision. Copper accepted his renewed, if somewhat limited eyesight with equanimity. The psychological damage could only be measured by the person who knew him best. As a war-time nurse, Tookie had mended egos and heartaches during a World War of lost lives and limbs. As she arose ill-tempered to greet the day for the second time this morning, she administered the shock therapy she had used before to shake life into the living. "You are a changed man, Copper Jack, hard and bitter since the blindness. All of our friends have told me so in private. You have no emotion. The last time in your life you cried was over a dead pig. You are a changed man, I say. I will always love you, but you are not the kind man I married. And heaven help us, should you have a relapse, you are going to blow your brains out. You are just waiting for night to fall again."

4

A Reason for Living

With the armchair opposite hers deserted, Tookie kicked impatiently at the floor with her bedroom slippers and mumbled several "bloody hells" under her breath. She spiked her cup of coffee with brandy and settled into her armchair to clear her head of cobwebs. She was actually disappointed when the front door opened and it was not Copper Jack.

"Apologies for walking in on you like this. Just saw Copper's car heading toward the bodega. So I figured you would be all alone this morning and in need of company."

"You only brought me home after church last night, Bilkington, because I got a bit tipsy. Let's not pretend you got lucky. We are too old for that anyway."

"Rubbish. But if that's supposed to be our storyline, so be it. The age of chivalry dies with me." Tookie poured him coffee. However, she was careful to steer Bustle toward the sofa and away from Copper's empty armchair.

"We had another serious row this morning."

"Probably explains why I saw Copper speeding out of control along the cliffs just now."

"You know, Bilkington, he flinches at the wheel ever so often when he drives. Someday he will kill us both if he doesn't kill himself first," she predicted, adding more brandy to her coffee for good measure.

"He hasn't been the same since the accident, I hear."

"It has never been a tea party, living with Copper. He's such a proud man. Never shares much of himself. He will adopt a stray kitten and make idle conversation with a total stranger. Yet try living with him. Like a whore, I don't even know the man I sleep with after all these years."

"Always wondered what you saw about him in the first place. Seemed completely daft you running away with a stoic pig farmer."

"How like you to be so short-sighted in your observations of everyone around you, Bilkington. Copper Jack could have become so many things: a Member of Parliament, a star rugby player, a real estate baron. Sad to say it's all passed him by now," she acknowledged.

"He still has you, which is far more than I have."

"Problem is, he doesn't need me and would be the first to tell you so. Always said his biggest mistake in life was marrying a woman with ambition. Lady Macbeth, he calls me. And without being able to have children of our own, I didn't even make a man out of him." Tookie paused, realized she had been talking to herself more than Bustle, and changed the direction of the conversation. "Excuse me, Bilkington, for going on like this. I'm not being very civil this morning. I did hear about your dear brother and all, most unfortunate. And how's Mrs Bustle, by the way? I'm sure you know the talk all over the Algarve is about you and Frill Pimpton."

Bustle recoiled from the comment. "The missus is losing touch and Frill is hitting the bottle. And you? Still lovely, still my one and only love and always will be," he professed, "and I refuse to believe otherwise no matter what you say."

"After all these years, you still have the audacity to hold out hope for us, you with a missus and a mistress?"

"Until I have you at my side, my life simply will not be complete," Bustle insisted, raising his cup of coffee in a mock toast. "To the two of us."

To chase away the demons of winter, Copper Jack gunned his car along the highway that ran parallel to, and within a stone's throw, of the original road to the bodega. The old road snakes along the rock cliffs precariously before losing its way altogether. It is no more than an ill-trodden path today where lizards scratch their bellies indecently. Copper eased off the accelerator as he approached a donkey and its rider, who were both old enough to remember better days. In the old days, dozens of donkey carts like this one, oozing with overripe grapes, once inched along these cliffs in unison. Now the old rider travels the road alone and, out of stubbornness, he refuses to admit his generation is a dying one. He rides sidesaddle and, with his tired eyes, drinks in the familiar expanse of Atlantic Ocean with the same sense of wonder. To his donkey who wears blinkers so he will not become startled and hurtle them both to their deaths, it is a world still pretty much the same.

Farther down the road, Copper's one good eye spied a squadron of gannets. They were licking their chops one last time and flying low over the coastline of Portugal before heading south for the winter. Suddenly, and in mass, they hurtled toward the ocean splashing the water frenetically around a school of fish. By the time the last gannet had his fill and returned to the squadron's flight pattern, Portuguese fishermen paddled their boats feverishly toward the same area, casting their nets in desperation, hoping to catch a few stray fish of their own.

Far above the village from her bedroom window on Millionaire Hill, Mrs Bustle also followed the flight of the gannets with her binoculars. She rarely missed any of the comings and goings of the Algarve from her favorite perch on the balcony. Her binoculars followed closely Copper's car speeding toward the bodega as it passed her husband's car speeding just as quickly in the opposite direction toward Tookie Jack's house.

The binoculars had been a harmless birthday present from Bustle. Something constructive to occupy his wife's senile brain, he decided, small pleasures for small minds. He also gave her several picture books about the birds of southern Portugal. Through her new binoculars, she recognized them all. She learned their habits intimately.

The sight she had anticipated all morning finally came into view and Mrs Bustle retired from the balcony and put her binoculars away for the day. Virgo's silver Citroen pulled into the long, winding driveway for the very first time and, like a rat in a maze, finally managed to arrive at the front door of the villa on the hill. Virgo stepped from the car wearing a scanty tennis outfit and clutching her bag of tricks. "Great day for tennis, don't you think?" Virgo winked, although Mrs Bustle did not return the gesture.

"Bilkington's safely on the golf course by now and I gave the maid the day off," she announced. All alone in the house, they climbed the stairway to her bedroom together. "I suppose my telephone call caught you off guard," said Mrs Bustle. "You know what I mean, coming from a lady of stature."

"Nothing about the Algarve surprises me anymore. More surprised you haven't called before now, actually."

When they reached the bedroom, Virgo continued on outside to the balcony. She looked admiringly across the mansions of other prominent customers she had conquered along the way. She returned to the bedroom to find Mrs Bustle nervously shutting off the bedroom lights and drawing the window blinds closed. "Are you sure we must do this in the dark, deary? It will just make things a bit more awkward. At least let me find the electrical outlet for the vibrator first," she said, removing the instrument from her bag.

With the lights dimmed, Mrs Bustle lay down on her back and stared up at the ceiling trying to conjure up seductive images of her husband. Virgo approached the frail, bird-like body with a growing sense of pity. Mrs Bustle trembled visibly in the shadows that fell across the bed. With Virgo's deft guiding hand, the vibrator massaged Mrs Bustle's private parts, arousing sensations she had never discovered before. Suddenly Mrs Bustle heard a growl and thought an animal had entered the room. In fact, what she heard was her own deep-throated, guttural shout of joy in a voice so foreign to her, yet so overcome with pleasure.

When the session was finally over, Virgo returned to the balcony to catch some fresh air. She drew back her hair and straightened herself against a breeze suddenly cold and biting. Mrs Bustle lingered in the shadows of sin for a while longer knowing the return of daylight would cast guilt over her actions, and the longer she remained spellbound by the intense feelings she had just experienced, the deeper the guilt would settle over her soul.

Without Bustle's love and affection, this grotesque cloakroom perversion was something she knew she would risk again.

Pulling his car into the parking lot of the bodega, Copper arrived too early for a drink. Liz poured tea at the bar for a bed and breakfast crowd of mostly Europeans, who had bothered to brave the damp Algarve winter in search of a lost weekend. Because of the deep dampness that settled into the bed-sheets this time of year, all her guests rose early to warm their bodies by the fire and steam their nostrils with several cups of hot tea.

As a local, Copper felt obliged to apologize about the bad weather to any house guest within earshot. "Not quite the same place this time of year," he acknowledged to no one in particular.

"None of your cryptic remarks in front on my guests," Liz whispered, standing on her orange crate behind the bar and leaning forward to pour him tea. "Bad for business if you keep complaining about the weather." Liz was already the second woman to bite his head off this morning and the day had barely begun. "So, did Tookie finally make it home last night?"

"Didn't notice," he lied. "And where's the reverend? Must be another war of some kind we can celebrate today."

"Same sermon, different congregation; Patrick's in Praia de Luz today, Portimao tomorrow, Albufiera the day after that. Had you any sense or respect of history, you would have attended the sermon yesterday along with the rest of us."

"No matter what fairy tales you used to tell your university students, Liz, English history is nothing more than a legacy of kings and queens gorging themselves while the people starved, spreading their legs for their own delight and making war whenever they became suddenly bored with one another. Total debauchery, nothing more, and all modern man does is repeat these stupidities of history."

"If mankind is as despicable as you say, why is your sitting room at home always overrun with these same people?"

"Because Tookie needs the attention I don't give her."

"Balls! Don't use your wife as an excuse. You are as lonely as the rest of us, Copper Jack. The reverend needs his congregation. I need the customers at my bar and you need all those sorry souls who populate your sitting room.

Warm bodies wander in, drink our liquor and steal our hearts with a tale or two, like Chaucer's pilgrims on the way to Canterbury. Sometimes," she philosophized, "I even delude myself into thinking I'm actually needed here on this earth."

"You are needed, Lizard," Copper agreed. "So how about a refill?"

"Then I catch myself and remember. It's me that needs them. With the reverend out of town so much of the time, most nights I crawl up those bloody stairs to bed all alone, after serving drinks into the wee hours to put it off as long as I can."

Becoming desperate to change the subject, Copper's eye drifted to the far end of the bar where a young man sat alone. After fighting side-by-side with Americans and bartering for their Hershey candy bars during the war, Copper could pick a Yank out of a crowd quicker than he could identify his own mother. And this one certainly fit the mold. He was broad-shouldered, naturally, with his blond head cocked to one side, seeing the world in his own unique way, inspired no doubt by some deep, quiet turmoil inside, which caused him to drink without really tasting, look without seeing, grin without smiling: preoccupied, instead, with rubbing his teacup restlessly between over-sized hands, as if the cup was an Aladdin's lamp waiting for the genie to escape and reveal the secrets of life.

"Two more teas, Lizard," Copper ordered, motioning to the end of the bar where he took a seat next to the American. "I don't understand your game of football," Copper said, by way of introduction. "No one cares where the ball is. Everyone's got their own private spat going all over the field. They come out wearing all that bloody gear, like Roman gladiators. It seems the object of the game is nothing more than to beat the stuffing out of your opponent."

"You seem to understand our game well enough," the American grinned.

"Enough to know if you brought your best football team to Wales, stripped them of their helmets and padding and placed them on a rugby field, we'd bloody hell run circles around your boys."

It didn't take the American long to respond. "Unfortunately, running around in circles and short pants doesn't score touchdowns. That's why America had to pitch in against Hitler: to teach Britain how to advance." Copper was suddenly enjoying himself too much to take the stinging comment personally.

"Obviously, you are too young to have been there. Never let that stop a man from having an uninformed opinion. It's exactly this brashness that I love about Americans. You all act like John Wayne, a cowboy through and through, even if you don't know the horse's head from his ass. If you did indeed teach the Brits how to advance, lad, certainly we had to teach you how to do it without getting your fool heads shot off."

Liz intervened, suddenly protective of her handsome American customer. "His name's Smitty and he's our guest for the winter," as if these slim personal credentials would encourage Copper to back off. "He's a writer," she added.

"Pleasure to make your acquaintance, Yank," Copper said, finally offering an outstretched hand. "A writer? In all due respect, Smitty, hasn't our Rudyard Kipling already said everything meaningful there is to say? After Kipling, what could possibly be left for you to write about?"

"About people gorging themselves, spreading their legs and making war."

Copper smiled. "I'm starting to like this Yank, Lizard. Hope you didn't take my history lesson too seriously," he said to Smitty. "Just needed to vent my spleen and it did me good. That's what a pub's for, right Liz?" Copper stood up to leave and left some loose change on the bar. But Liz pushed it back at him as usual.

"Keeping you in debt to me keeps you coming back for more."

"So long as I don't put you in the poor house."

"You know I don't do it for anyone else but you."

"I'll be back," Copper reassured her.

After Copper left, Smitty stated the obvious. "You think a lot of him, don't you?"

"Maybe too much," Liz admitted.

On his way home from the bodega, Copper stopped to purchase a fresh bouquet of flowers from a retired Portuguese fisherman, who prefers selling flowers over fish in his old age. "Mr Bom Dia," as he was known to the villagers, could just as well go by the nickname "Mr Bom Tarde." Like every other retired fisherman from dawn to dusk, Mr Bom Dia spends his day chasing the sun and warming his bones on the sunny doorsteps across the village. He cushions his trouser bottoms with a scrap of cardboard he also carries with him for warmth against the cold concrete stoops. With friends and strangers alike, Mr Bom Dia chats endlessly.

He patronizes young children and old cronies like himself. He teases and flirts with the shriveled hags that labor by toting straw baskets miraculously on the tops of their heads. To the Portuguese, Mr Bom Dia is as much a part of village life as the church bell clanging every hour on the hour, the political graffiti fading from the village walls from the revolution, and the whimsical tide rising and falling against the shoreline. Yet, among the Englishmen, only Copper Jack paid him any notice, maybe because Mr Bom Dia was blind.

"For Senora Zack?" Mr Bom Dia guessed when Copper purchased the bouquet of flowers from him.

"For my sitting room," he insisted. Back in the driver's seat with the flowers in hand, as always Copper signed the card "His Majesty."

It had been so much easier to turn her back on Bustle that night on the dance floor many years ago. This time around, in the premises of her own sitting room, he held on to her tighter. Or perhaps Tookie just felt weaker.

"Tell me it's not too late for us," Bustle pleaded his case, holding her in his arms.

Just then, Copper Jack arrived. If Copper was startled by what he saw, he refused to show it. He held the inopportune bouquet of anemones behind his back until he could stuff them unnoticed into a nearby vase. Without breaking stride, Copper left the sitting room in favor of the open air of the veranda. He disappeared from sight before Tookie and Bustle could break awkwardly from their embrace. When Bustle finally ventured forth sheepishly to the veranda, Copper was ready for him.

"Copper, we were just reliving a wrong turn the two of us took on the dance floor many years ago," Bustle tried to explain.

"Meaning Tookie should have run away with you, not me."

"Precisely, and I think she knows that now."

"As always, your brains are between your legs, Bustle."

"Proud to say I still have something of substance between my legs, old chap."

Copper finished Bustle's thought. "And absolutely nothing whatsoever between your shoulder blades." As if to prove his point, Copper threw a punch trying to knock Bustle's head off and missed the mark. With one good eye, Copper was a better judge of character than distance. Before Copper could redeem himself and attempt a second punch, Tookie was on top of them both, pulling them apart like school children in a playground skirmish.

"Gentlemen! Gentlemen! Please do stop. Guests have arrived, including your wife, Bilkington," she announced with special irritation.

5

Piccadilly Circus

Mrs Bustle and Virgo sat in separate corners of the sofa, like matching bookends. Bustle, unfortunately, was obliged to sit between them.

"What a pleasant surprise," Tookie pretended, looking at the strange collection of visitors in her sitting room and trying to put a happy face on an otherwise awkward moment. "Gin and tonics all around," she announced, which she knew to be the perfect prescription, and no one in the room objected. As Tookie departed to retrieve the drinks, Bustle shot a partial smile her way before turning to face his wife.

"I was on my way to the golf course, my dear. Just thought I'd check in on Copper Jack to find out where his handicap stands these days since we haven't seen him on the course lately and we could certainly use some fresh blood at the Club." Bustle shot a stern look Copper's way, who returned it with a scowl of his own. "And what brings you here, my darling." Bustle's question was targeted to Virgo as much as it was his own wife.

"Mrs Bustle and I were on our way home after a few tennis lessons when we saw your car parked in Copper Jack's driveway," Virgo was quick to cover up.

"That's right," Mrs Bustle insisted, shaking her head in agreement with the clever alibi. Bustle seemed doubtful.

"Didn't realize you had taken up the sport, my dear," he said, so Virgo quickly came to her new client's defense.

"Such a civilized sport, don't you think?" opening up her question to the sitting room audience at large. "Sometimes I even think the game of tennis may well have been Britain's greatest contribution to the colonies. Don't you think, Copper Jack?"

"In India, I don't think Gandhi would have given us even that much credit, especially the part about being civilized."

Bustle, the former colonialist, flushed with indignation. "My god, Copper, how can you so willingly make such a bloody fool of yourself. After the war, you never touched foreign soil again in your life until you abducted Tookie to Portugal. I can't speak for India. Yet I can assure you first hand that our colonial presence in Africa actually protected tribe's from eating each other's flesh."

"In a part of the world where eating flesh is a perfectly accepted code of behavior," Copper noted.

"And no matter what that naked malcontent Gandhi said about our occupation of India," corrected Bustle, "we provided his peasants with just laws, favorable taxes, adequate irrigation, ample schools, protection from foreign states."

Copper quickly interrupted. "Exactly, everything we could never provide for our own island because we were too busy saving the rest of the world in our own image. All that rot about white man's burden, and to what end? By now Britain was supposed to be floating on a sea of rubies, elephant tusks and exotic spices. Instead, we're drowning in a sea of debt. We've become a second class world power overrun with foreigners. And with their British citizenship, they're quick to jump on welfare. Let's face it, Bustle. We all live in the Algarve because we got tired of paying taxes to support them."

"Bilkington built airports," Mrs Bustle injected belatedly, trying to come to her husband's defense.

"Runways," Bustle clarified, "near gold mines in dense African jungle, fighting off malaria every step of the way."

Copper remained unimpressed. "Made your fortune in kickbacks on the black market, I suspect."

"In Africa, what other color would the marketplace be?" Bustle joked. Copper couldn't resist digging the knife in deeper.

"And all the while you were happily on the payroll in service to your Queen and country, turns out you were bilking both the UK and Africa at the same time."

Even in the face of harsh criticism, Bustle maintained an unflappable air of superiority. "Show me a civil servant living on Millionaire Hill who could have retired here comfortably without fiddling an income on the side."

"With the likes of you in charge of expanding our empire, it's a wonder Gandhi remained a pacifist."

"There was nothing passive whatsoever about the African Zulus, old chap, I assure you. Of course, you were off tending to a few pigs in Kent instead of serving your country abroad." Bustle welcomed Tookie's sudden return to the sitting room. He was thirsty and hoped he could direct his comments to a more sympathetic audience. "Must be difficult being married to a saint," Bustle concluded, accepting a gin and tonic and not waiting for a toast.

"Especially when he sits here all day in judgment from his armchair, like god almighty," she agreed. "Frankly, I'm fed up with Copper's political views. My response these days is usually: 'And what hast thou done about it?' And, of course, he's done nothing."

"Afraid I'm to blame for this little dust-up, Tookie," Virgo confessed. "Believe it or not, I got all this started simply by bringing up the game of tennis."

"And I shall wash the nonsense away as I always do," Tookie announced, downing her gin and tonic in a single breath.

"I do miss those days, Bilkington," Mrs Bustle blurted out suddenly. She lagged several sentences behind in the conversation, as usual. "We've tried so hard to make our life here in the Algarve as rich as it was in Africa. It's just not the same."

Bustle was as annoyed as much by his wife's bad timing as he was by her utter lack of substance. "I don't know what you're talking about. Not sure you do either anymore."

"You remember," Mrs Bustle reminded him, sounding exasperated. "The Club, the servants, the princely tiger shoots you loved so dearly."

Bustle tried his best to change the subject and prevent further character damage to himself. "You're dwelling on the past and boring everyone to death. It's a bloody nuisance looking into the rear view mirror."

"Memories are a great comfort to me these days," she confided, almost whispering. Tookie tried to sound sympathetic to Mrs Bustle's cause.

"Recalling good memories is probably healthier than trying to drink away the bad ones. And anything's better than sitting around playing bridge all day. As we all know, life can get awfully dull in the Algarve."

"Which is part of the reason I stopped by, Tookie," Virgo said. "Thought you might be so bored I could interest you in some tennis lessons or a bit of massage sometime." Virgo's comment set off a sudden chuckle from Copper Jack.

"You would certainly have a formidable project on your hands, Virgo, trying to whip this specimen of my wife into shape. I've long since forgotten what a trim pair of hips should look like."

Of course, Tookie did not back down, standing up from her armchair at six-foot tall and moving ominously closer to Copper. As if to punctuate her words, she put both her hands boldly on her huge, stately hips. "More to the point, Copper, you have long since forgotten what to do with a shapely pair of hips. And what kind of physical specimen are you? You don't tuck your shirt inside your pants when you bother to get dressed at all, which means our poor guests have to look at your disgusting belly hang out." At close range, Tookie noticed

Copper's day-old whiskers, the final indignation. "Look at you! You haven't even bothered to shave today!" she exclaimed, stomping her foot on the hardwood floor for emphasis.

"Anyone feel that earthquake?" Copper asked his guests, bobbing and weaving side-to-side, mimicking a quaking motion from the safety of his armchair. Tookie was finished with Copper for the time being and directed her comments to Virgo.

"Thanks for the offer, Virgo. As you can see, all the romance in my life is gone. What motivation do I have to get into shape and suddenly look ravishing?"

"Personally, I'd like to know Virgo's secret of success," said Bustle, ogling over the delightful pair of alabaster knees showing beneath her short tennis skirt.

"She's half our age," Tookie said, stating the obvious.

"Besides, I have no secrets," Virgo lied.

"Well, as for me, I feel fit as a fiddle."

"And how do you do it at your age, Bilkington?" Virgo asked. "What's your secret," she couldn't resist asking.

"Thought you'd never ask," he responded, always delighted to bear public witness to his vitality. "I fish from the rocks by day with my shirt off and read Shakespeare with a good brandy at night. Several years ago some orthopedist in the UK who makes a hobby of collecting patellas from people our age, wanted to have a go at my knees. I simply told him to bugger off. Sure I waddle a bit like a penguin, and don't we all at our age. So I kept my patellas to myself and last year I even practiced with the local Portuguese football team without hurting myself. In short, I'm six decades old and want for nothing," Bustle said proudly.

In the face of so much vanity, Copper couldn't help but share his disgust. "Sounds like you literally have life by the balls, Bustle," he said, striking a nerve.

"Then why do you insist on making it sound like a kick in the balls every time you address me!"

Finally, Tookie intervened again. "Gentlemen! Gentlemen! And I do use the term loosely. If you just put down your bows and arrows, I'll get us all another round of drinks."

"Pax," Bustle offered.

"Pox to you," Copper countered.

"Like you anyway, old chap. Just wish you wouldn't lose your sense of humor." Just then two more guests arrived at the front door uninvited.

"Liz, what a surprise to see you!" Tookie exclaimed, trying to sound upbeat with the arrival of yet another adversary.

"Don't know why it should be. I close up the bodega after siesta because the Portuguese all return to work. The Jack's house is the only bar that stays open this late in the afternoon," she joked, while Tookie was suddenly more interested by the young stranger at her side.

"Isn't this one awfully young for you, Liz?"

"Probably explains why he hasn't made a pass at me yet. Tookie, meet Smitty, my American house guest at the bodega this winter."

"An American? Is there a war on? Just kidding, Yank. Come ahead. You're always welcome here."

"Liz and her new boyfriend," was how Tookie introduced them as they all entered the sitting room.

"Don't recognize you without your orange crate, Lizard," teased Bustle. Copper stood up from his armchair to greet his two new guests. "Always glad to welcome a couple of civilized souls into these otherwise unruly tea-parties my wife likes to host."

Liz introduced Smitty to Virgo. "She's our local masseuse and astrologer. Dressed for tennis, I see. By the way, Smitty, you and Virgo are nearly roommates at the bodega."

Virgo pressed Smitty's hand meaningfully.

"Haven't yet had the pleasure," Smitty said.

"Perhaps you will," Virgo smiled without blinking an eye.

"Welcome to Piccadilly Circus, Smitty," Tookie said finally, cutting Virgo short and offering her American guest a chair next to hers. "These tea-parties, as Copper likes to call them, are part of the Algarve's answer to Piccadilly Circus. Have you ever been to London, Smitty? No matter, I've never been to the States either," Tookie admitted.

"Although," Copper added, "we did find out recently Tookie has a ninety-year-old aunt in the State's who's in prison there for stabbing her husband in the back. We were instructed we could mail her letters to Trap Six in care of San Quentin." Everyone laughed at the story except Tookie.

"Isn't it improper for Copper to talk about my aunt like that? We don't really have any of the details about what led up to the murder. Only that Aunt Nell apparently did him in. Serves him right from what I remember. Aunt Nell probably had it up to here with the way he crunched his toast at breakfast every morning for sixty years."

Copper couldn't resist. "That's why you won't find me crunching my toast or turning my back on Tookie anymore. This back-stabbing business could prove to be hereditary."

Liz interjected finally on behalf of her guest. "Smitty, are you beginning to see why I dragged you along? I promised to show Smitty some of the sights and sounds of the Algarve. He's a writer, after all."

Smitty glanced at Copper. "Not Kipling, of course."

"God forbid you should be as stuffy and self-righteous as Rudyard," Tookie said, taking exception to the comparison. "Besides, being American, I'm sure you have already observed your very own Peyton Place is playing out before your very eyes right here in the Algarve."

Liz offered Smitty her own perspective. "If you haven't guessed by now, Smitty, talk to Tookie if you ever need to know what's happening in the Algarve. She keeps her ear to the grapevine. When you start to feel cut off from the real world, talk to Copper. He listens to the wireless."

"And anything else you need to know, Bilkington Bustle is forever at your service," he said, standing up and taking a bow. "Which reminds me, Smitty, in the sight-seeing you've done so far, have you seen the rather crude-looking statue of Portugal's youngest king standing proudly in the center of the village roundabout?"

Smitty nodded his head. "It's hard to miss."

Tookie agreed. "It is an awful sight. They cracked the mold when they made that one. A by-product of melted down sardine cans, I should think." Liz seconded the motion.

"The wise man is not the one who sculpted the work, it's the person who managed to sell it to the Portuguese authorities."

Finally, Bustle took control back of the conversation. "No more side issues, ladies. Smitty, the real importance of the statue is not its historic or artistic value at all. What is important is that the Club has just promised a thousand pounds to any chap willing and able enough to pinch the king's crown under the cover of night. Unfortunately, the king is maybe 20 feet tall, so I'm afraid the job will require a three-man team. I'm willing to be top-man on the human totem pole and take full responsibility for any difficulties we may encounter with the authorities. Smitty, you look like a young, sturdy lad, certainly not as brittle as the rest of us. You should have spine enough to boost two old farts on top of your shoulders. Will you be my anchor man?"

"What's the plan?" Smitty asked with a degree of skepticism.

"We won't attempt it until midnight under a full moon. We'll sort through the details of the plan by killing off a few pints back at Casa Bodega after dinner to bolster our courage."

"So, if I agree to anchor, who's the third person between you and me?" Bustle turned to Copper Jack.

"Copper, would you agree to be the middle man? Our disagreements aside, there's no one I would trust more on a dangerous mission than a military man. What do you say? A thousand pounds split three ways?"

"Keep your money, Bustle. Would I miss out on an opportunity to help you break your neck? I would miss my own funeral first and Smitty will be on hand to write your obituary."

"Jolly good. It's settled then. Tookie, how about another round of drinks, if you would be so kind? I believe a toast is in order." Bustle had that marvelous feeling again, that is, until Frill Pimpton opened the front door without knocking and invited herself into the sitting room.

"Am I several rounds behind?" she asked rhetorically.

"Breathe on me darling and I'll let you know," Tookie answered snidely before leaving the room to fetch some more booze.

So, there you have it. Under one roof the fates had conspired to unite Bustle's complete menagerie of women: his wife, his mistress and his one and only love. Even Bilkington Bustle had to admit three women were probably excessive for a man his age. As painful as the admission was, he decided the best way to narrow the field was by letting the women compete for his favors. Give equal access to them all and let the chips fall where they may.

When Tookie delivered the fresh round of drinks, Bustle offered a toast. "Duo Vivimus Vivimus," he said, raising his glass above his head. "Let us live while we live."

6

"Had We Never Lov'd Sae Blindly"

Siesta dwindled down into dusk. Under the guiding light of the moon, the entourage stumbled along from Jack's villa and arrived at the bodega shortly after Liz opened the doors for dinner. From every café along the way the night wailed with laments of the fado, ancient Portuguese melodies mourning the loss of better days gone by, translated into the depth and breadth of a single, all-encompassing word: "Fate."

Safely inside Casa Bodega the Three Musketeers, Bilkington, Copper and Smitty settled into a table in the far corner where they could swig on a few pints of ale and tempt fate by making plans to pinch the king's crown later that night. Tookie, Mrs Bustle and Frill chose a dinner table much closer to the entertainment, where they could hear close up the singer's tortured whines and agonizing falsettos as well as the aggravated chords of his fellow guitarist.

After going upstairs and changing into an evening gown, Virgo headed toward the table to join the three women. On the way, she nodded to several of her clients, who were also present. The tables were full of familiar faces from Millionaire Hill, more women than men, more lonely than not. Most of their husbands had passed away, left town on business, or simply preferred the company of other men at the Club and the women, it seems, always preferred listening to the fado.

Two Portuguese winos sat at the bar scratching their day-old whiskers and counting their blessings. The lure of the full moon and the enchantment of the fado had brought the English senoras out in full force. They knew the middle-aged Portuguese singer, with dark greasy hair wearing a rented tuxedo, would get first choice of the women. His aging guitarist would get second choice.

Even the pair of toothless winos knew they were pretty good bets to find a partner for the night.

During the dinner rush hour, Liz's frizzy-haired head was rarely visible above the bar countertop. She had to abandon her trusty orange crate as she divided her time racing back and forth between mixing drinks at the bar and shouting instructions to the kitchen. After the crowds were all gone, however, she was the best bet at night's end to crawl under her eiderdown all alone. The reverend was out of town and in his absence Liz had always been eternally faithful. As much as any widow or jilted lover, Liz identified with the fado's lament.

Bustle, Copper and Smitty ironed out the details of their secret mission just as they finished up dinner. So the trio decided to settle into bar stools to keep Liz good company until midnight.

"Here's a smug looking group," Liz acknowledged.

"Dinner hour is over, Liz. Pull up your orange crate for a visit," Copper insisted. Bustle pushed his empty beer mug towards her.

"Just focus on making sure we're well stocked for the night to keep our courage up."

"If I'm able to get you good and tight, maybe you'll call off this silly mischief. You would be bonkers even to try it sober," she admonished them.

"If it will make you feel better, Liz, I promise to wear the crown to the bodega first before I ever don it at the Club and collect my winnings."

"You will wear it straight to the clink, Bustle," Liz predicted. "Just don't call in the middle of the night expecting me to empty the till and post your bail money." She gave Copper a concerned look.

"Not to worry, Liz. I'm the designated adult tonight," Copper reassured her. "My job's to keep us out of harm's way."

Suddenly, Bustle grew animated, gesturing wildly toward the dining room where the ladies all swooned in unison with each cry of the fado. "Would you look at this? More witches flying around here than on Halloween night. Liz, when the night is over, do you plan to fly them back to Millionaire Hill on broomsticks, or bed them all here in one mass orgy?"

"I run a respectable business, Bustle, except when you're on the premises." Bustle tapped Smitty on the shoulder.

"So, which lady do you prefer, my young Lochinvar? I can fix you up with any of them," he boasted. Bolstered by the beer, Smitty didn't hesitate.

"How about Virgo?"

"Not so hasty, lad, take a second look. Seated nearest the singer we have Mrs Yorkshire, recently widowed, drops coins down her cleavage to attract suitors. Moving clockwise, we have the Queen of Persia, a nickname, the one with the gargantuan boobs cradled on the edge of her dining room table – wears gowns slit up to her thighs and throws kitchen dishes at her twit of a husband. He's a weed and a cuckold and looks the other way.

"Next, we have Mrs Chippendale, the one with her elbow in her soup, drinks as heavily as Frill and, as you can see, is already very far along this evening. Her diamonds are for real, by the way, and the fur coat is no imitation either. So if you're more interested in money than sex, she's the obvious choice."

When the fado finally came to an end, the audience applauded eagerly as the Portuguese singer took several deep bows. Bustle could not help but envy the singer because every bare knee in the joint was pointed in his direction and the thigh-high stockings were all open for business. The two Portuguese winos at the bar slobbered on themselves in anticipation of what was to come next.

"They all want fucking," Bustle muttered.

"You're starting to repeat yourself, Bustle," Liz complained.

"Must be contagious," he said, glowering across the dining room at Mrs Bustle, who seemed to him to be having too much of a good time. "That's why, Yank, it's good to have you here in the Algarve for a while. We have all run out of things to say to one another. No wonder we repeat ourselves."

It was intermission and time for the entertainers to take a break. The singer excused himself from his captive audience in the dining room and passed the bar on his way to the men's room. A shot of brandy was waiting for him at the end of the bar.

"Obrigada, senora," he said, raising his glass in a toast to the bartender, and downing the brandy in one gulp before disappearing into the bathroom.

"He gets better service than we do," Bustle complained to Liz.

"Jose is prettier than you. Besides, as you can see, he keeps my customers coming back for more."

"I agree he's one immaculate son of a bitch, a chromosome away from nipples, if you ask me, and most certainly the bladder of a woman."

Soon the singer returned from the bathroom, downed another brandy Liz had poured for him at the end of the bar, and never broke stride as he returned confidently to his adoring fans waiting in the dining room.

"Struts around in that tuxedo like a bloody matador," Bustle complained.

"You're just jealous, Bustle," Copper noted. "Mrs Bustle doesn't seem to be complaining."

"Well passed her bedtime, actually, must run the missus home before she gets herself into trouble. Smitty, Copper, I'll meet you two gentlemen at the village roundabout half past midnight."

After Bustle's sudden departure, Smitty excused himself for the evening as well. He noticed Virgo leave the dining room and head up their stairway toward her room. He debated with himself whether to intercept her. For the moment, Liz and Copper were left alone.

"Everything all right with you, Copper Jack?" Liz asked with genuine concern. Copper scoffed.

"Isn't that asking a lot out of life at our advanced age?"

"Something's definitely not been right with you lately."

"Just the arrival of winter," he said.

"Sure it's not Tookie and Bustle, more than the change in seasons, that's put you in this funk?" she asked. Copper shook his head no. "Then how's your eyesight fairing these days?"

Copper tried to reassure Liz by forcing a grin and making a joke. "I see well enough to realize the Queen of Prussia's got way too much for me to satisfy. And what about you, Lizard?" he asked.

"Frankly, I'm worried, Copper Jack. Nothing wrong with growing old, just don't like feeling old."

"Sounds like Reverend Pat's got you working too hard."

"No, it's deeper than that. Only brought up the idea just in case you might be feeling the same way I do." Copper lit a cigarette and looked away from Liz.

"In a different way, perhaps," was all he said before lapsing into another prolonged silence. Finally, Liz was beside herself.

"Well for God's sake, Copper, talk to me about how you really feel then." Copper took another monotonous drag from his cigarette and exhaled deeply, as if some small corner of his life had just expired.

"Don't much mind growing old, just don't care for the notion of being forgotten. Seems like such a damn waste of a lifetime. No children to remember me by – and no one's going to erect a statue of me. Suppose that's why I'm going along with Bustle's shenanigans later tonight. I rather respect the old king's longevity."

"You know what Patrick says. After we're gone, Copper, our spirits carry on."

"This life is hard enough. Why would anyone hope to carry on when it's all over, retracing steps already taken, reliving mistakes best forgotten?" he asked. "No thanks, just spread the sod over me and bloody well be done with it."

Liz understood Copper well enough not to go there.

With Virgo and Mrs Bustle both excusing themselves and leaving the dining room table for the evening, Tookie was left to direct a few tactless questions toward Frill Pimpton. "You seem to be coping remarkably well, my dear. I mean with Freddy passing on and all. Bilkington must be a great comfort to you at a time like this."

"One does what one must do in times like this, don't we Tookie?" she asked in an equally accusatory tone.

"But you would appear to do it so much better. Or is it just that no man gets turned away from Frill Pimpton's bed?"

"Why is my bedroom suddenly your business?"

"Because Bilkington says he loves me." Frill did not try to stifle a wicked little laugh.

"Bilkington loves no one except himself."

"And still you don't turn him away?"

"I don't need love anymore. And I don't have a man like Copper Jack to lean on even if I did." Tookie sounded disgusted.

"Makes me so furious, everyone thinks Copper is such a peach."

"Then count me as one of them. You'd be an absolute fool to let that man get away, especially for Bustle. If you can't see that, you're the one who's blind, not Copper. I would take him off your hands in a blink of the eye."

"I'll make it easy for you, then. How about a simple exchange, Copper for Bustle?"

As if to seal their wicked, secret pact, they clinked their wine glasses together harmlessly.

Virgo was turning the doorknob to her upstairs room at the bodega when Smitty approached from the other end of the hallway. "What a coincidence to meet you here," Smitty remarked. "Guess our rooms are actually just across the hall from one another."

"That's why I'm surprised I haven't heard your typewriter lately."

"Didn't realize you could hear it, Virgo. Sorry if my typing disturbs you," he apologized.

"Only when the typing stops do I worry. The sound has become welcomingly familiar. For some reason, I have come to depend on it." Smitty blushed before explaining his recent silence.

"Just came up for a little air lately. I'll get back to it," he promised.

Virgo invited Smitty into her room and motioned for him to take a seat on her sofa.

"So, what are you writing about so passionately," she asked, sitting close enough to him to smell his aftershave. When Smitty didn't answer, she took a slightly different tack. "OK, then. Shall we talk about what brought you to Portugal in the first place? Or is that part of the story also off limits?"

"I didn't come here to talk, that's for sure," he said, standing up suddenly as if he was about to leave.

"Sit down," Virgo insisted. "If you won't talk, I'll just have to guess," she said, smiling. Smitty sat down again on the sofa next to Virgo as he allowed this total stranger to prick his curiosity. At least her evening gown caught his attention. It fell open at the front whenever she crossed her legs, revealing the full length of her legs from ankle to thigh. "My guess is you are not a writer at all, just some kind of imposter. More likely you were stepped on by a woman and it hurt. You had to get far away."

For now, Smitty was content to play along with her game. "Sounds like you've been reading my mail," he teased.

"Don't have to, actually. Just reading your eyes tells me everything I need to know. I also read fortunes. Give me your palm, if you're man enough."

"Will I get it back?"

"Don't worry. I have places to put your hand for safe keeping." Smitty was close enough to smell her perfume and read her eyes as well. Virgo took his palm into her own hands confidently, without ever getting his permission. "You have a pronounced lifeline. Turns out you will meet someone very important to your life. In fact, it's highly likely you have already met this mysterious person." Virgo paused a moment to let the idea sink in, but Smitty was having none of it.

"Come on, Virgo. I could get that much wisdom from a fortune cookie." Smitty leaned forward trying to find her lips, yet Virgo playfully pushed him away. Smitty pretended to be indignant. "So, you are just teasing. Like all the English, your tongue is squarely in your cheek at all times. Everything you say and do is pure posturing."

"Yes, and you Americans are always so charmingly earnest and straightforward, like an open book," she chided him.

"Just like to know where I stand, that's all," he said, standing up for a second time as if to leave.

"If you keep leaving my room, cowboy, we will never get to know one another." Virgo calmly filled two glasses from a wine bottle on the table in front of them. Smitty was again persuaded to take a seat.

"What's with the constant cowboy reference, anyway? Copper does the same thing."

"All Americans seem like cowboys to the English. Right or wrong, it's the image we get from your motion pictures," she explained.

"Maybe you should visit the States sometime and try to broaden your horizons."

"What? And get killed by your mafia?" Virgo started to laugh, only cut it short in time to gently admonish herself and her countrymen for the stereotypes. "I know. You're absolutely right. My tongue is once again in my cheek."

Smitty decided a little role reversal was in order. "Now that you think you've uncovered a few of my secrets, what about yours?" he asked and Virgo never hesitated.

"The guesses I made about your life are actually true about mine."

"About getting stepped on, hurt? And then meeting an important person?" Virgo nodded her head, fell back against a pillow on the end of the couch and propped a bare leg and one of her high heels on the edge of the coffee table, just enough for Smitty to get a glimpse of eternity.

"It must get terribly lonely being so far from home," she said.

Her black mesh stockings were the old-fashioned kind made famous by barmaids and vaudeville dancers. The dark seam on the back of each leg lifted his eyes as high on the thigh as he dared to look. The stockings ended abruptly with a colorful garter which pinched the flesh pink on the thigh and seemed to warn: 'No trespassing beyond this point'.

"I want you," Virgo whispered softly, reaching across the couch and pulling Smitty on top of her. Downstairs at Casa Bodega, the fado was reaching a feverish pitch.

During Jose's next musical number, he mingled among his fans in the dining room. As things heated up, an open shirt collar replaced his bow tie, showing off ample tufts of sweaty black chest hair. Occasionally, he would bow and kiss the ladies' hands that were thrust his way, study the cleavage at point blank range, and whisper sensual encouragement in Portuguese. Mrs Yorkshire, as if on cue, dropped more coins down her bra than a popular penny arcade could possibly absorb at one time. Beneath the table and discretely out of sight, the Queen of Persia dropped one of her high heels to the floor and brushed against Jose's ankle with her stockinged foot. The two Portuguese winos smiled smugly at one another at the bar.

"Looks like the Queen of Persia's got the inside track," Copper observed, as if to handicap the competition for Liz who watched the proceedings with rapt attention.

"She always gets her man," Liz agreed.

Two early drop outs from the competition, Tookie and Frill, staggered over to the bar for some solace, licking their wounds and slurring their words. "I have to say, Liz, at the bodega you run quite the supermarket" Frill offered. "Bed and breakfast, pub and restaurant, church every Sunday, masseuse always on call, even a Portuguese gigolo for lady's night out on the town."

"Tookie didn't embarrass herself tonight, did she," Copper asked Frill.

"No. I didn't embarrass you, Copper," Tookie answered, not even bothering to look his way or acknowledge his presence.

"If you have to ask how your wife behaved, your eyesight must really be failing you," Frill said.

"Don't be a sore loser, Frill, by attacking others," Liz responded.

"Actually, I'm the real winner tonight. Tookie said I could have Copper Jack. Isn't that so, Tookie?"

"Straightaway, as far as I'm concerned," she said, more interested in keeping her eyes riveted to the action in the dining room.

"Can I drop you home, Frill?" Copper offered.

"It's true then? You are all mine?" she seemed surprised.

"Actually, I need to take Tookie home," Copper corrected Frill politely. "We could drop you off on our way." Of course, Tookie would have none of it.

"Do what you please with your evening, Copper Jack. As for me, I'm just warming up," she announced. "Another gin and tonic, Liz."

"How about just tonic water this time?" Liz suggested.

"You think I'm tight and can't hold my liquor. Make it a double gin and tonic, then, just to show you what I'm made of." Copper stood up suddenly as if to leave, except Tookie wasn't budging. "You really expect me to go home with you?" Tookie asked, turning to confront her husband for the first time all evening. "You without any teeth in your head? How many times have I begged you to go have the dentist put in a set of pearly whites just like the American actor, Burt Lancaster?" Copper glared back at her motionless with his arms folded at his sides and, as Tookie said, she was just warming up for a soliloquy. "Furthermore, you have been wearing the same pair of socks for several days now."

"I tried to change recently, didn't I? I couldn't find a matching pair thanks to how you mismanage the laundry."

"Your shoes want polishing—"

"—these are slippers."

"Your face wants shaving—"

"—you never kiss me anymore."

"And when we get home you will expect me to crawl into bed and kiss your vacuum cleaner mouth goodnight."

"A handshake, then," Copper acquiesced, as he began to surrender under the onslaught of her diatribe.

"Then, in the middle of the night, you will snore through an open mouth of nicotine breath, pass some unfortunate stomach gas, scratch my ankles with your toenails that want clipping, hog most the blanket and all of the hot water bottle, before rising with insomnia at four o'clock in the morning to listen to the wireless until I finally get tired of hearing your stomach growl and get out of bed to make breakfast," she concluded, completely out of breath and even more worked up than before.

Copper had a better idea. "Why don't we just stay awake all night long and avoid this unpleasantness of going to bed?" After another deep swig of gin and tonic, Tookie's rant resumed unabated.

"And when I finally get out of bed in the morning, you will try to greet me with a kiss of whiskers that will surely scratch my face, suck in my lips with your dishrag mouth, and say something absolutely stupid like: 'Darling, I think you're gorgeous.' Well, I'm completely fed up, I tell you."

"That's because you are gorgeous," Copper agreed, "although you are clearly not having one of your better days. Fortunately, for you and for everyone else, the day is almost over," Copper decided, lifting Tookie up suddenly and throwing her over his shoulder clumsily like a sack of potatoes that would bruise if dropped. The full evening of nonstop drinking forced the alcohol to rush to Tookie's head, which took away all the remaining fight left in her. "When you see him, Liz, tell the Yank I'll be back to pick him up," Copper shouted back, as he pushed open the bodega doors and escaped into the moonlit night.

Balanced across his sagging shoulder blade, the full weight of Tookie teetered precariously in the arms of Copper Jack.

Mrs Bustle spent most evenings alone in bed reviewing over and over again the family photo album perched reassuringly on her lap, a collection of images and memories from the distant days of their life in Africa, a point in time to her that seemed as vivid as yesterday. Bustle would leave his wife perfumed, frilled and ready for bed, still not quite ready for the solitude that fell like the final curtain every time Bustle left her alone. "Sleep tight, my darling," he would always say on his way out the door, knowing full well she rarely slept anymore.

Most early mornings he would return home from a night at the pub to find the television still going, with Mrs Bustle sitting upright in bed as wide-eyed as when he left her several hours earlier. If, finally, she ever managed to nod off, the family photo album was always open faithfully on her lap. Bustle had a scheduled date with a statue in the village roundabout and was determined tonight's exit strategy would be no different.

"Sleep tight, my darling," he said on his way out the door.

"Please stay, Bilkington. Just a while longer," she begged.

"You alright, my sweet?" he asked, returning to her bedside impatiently.

"Hold me close, Bilkington," she pleaded with him. Suppose it would not do any harm, he decided, if it would help her sleep. He glanced at his wristwatch and decided he had a few minutes to spare. He took his shoes off and stretched out on the bed at her side. Bustle wrapped his broad arms around his wife's narrow shoulders and allowed her head to nestle under his chin.

There had never been talk of divorce between them. Even in retirement, a successful man of the world like Bustle, and a respected former colonialist, he was expected to have at his side a charming, loyal and obedient wife to help him maintain the proper social appearances. In his mind, the missus still filled the role well enough, except for an occasional lapse of senility and, although he could not admit to ever having loved her, Bustle still prided himself in the notion he had returned her loyalty in kind, if only in his mind, not his actions.

"Closer, Bilkington," she asked. When he squeezed, it was if all the air came out of her with a rush. "Oh, Bilkington!" she sobbed uncontrollably. For all the lapses of memory, Mrs Bustle remembered clearly what she loved most about her husband. Bustle was extremely alive, always had been, forever between this or in search of that. He constantly fidgeted his way through life as if he might miss out on something important if he didn't hurry. It didn't matter if, in the process, he actually missed out on a lot.

In her mind, Mrs Bustle believed that by hanging on to Bustle's unending enthusiasm, she would at least be able to share in his unusual zest for life. In truth, all she really achieved was to hang on desperately like a millstone around his neck, a fact Bustle never let her forget.

In the early morning hours of his sidewalk beat, Captain Baptiste leaned his back against the outside of the town bank, warmed his hands in his pockets, and played pocket polo with his privates to fight off boredom. Except for the statue of the Portuguese king in the center of the roundabout, the streets were deserted. No cars, no people. Even the fado had been put to sleep for the evening and all the cafes were empty.

Crime was never a problem in this sleepy village of Lagos. In fact, Captain Baptiste could not remember the last time he had reason to pull his gun from his holster. In a few minutes the Captain would be mercifully off duty and free to go to bed himself. Until then, there was nothing left for an officer of the law to do in the cold night air except to fiddle a pleasant erection in his pants for warmth, and to look forward to retiring soon to the arms of his loving wife.

When the church bell in the village tolled precisely at midnight, the silhouette of Bilkington Bustle under a full moon marched proudly into the center of the roundabout and stood defiantly in the shadow of the statue of the Portuguese king. His white alabaster shins, gleaming beneath his pleated Scottish kilt, lit up the night like the moon. Soon, he was not alone.

"Excuse me, Mrs Bustle," a voice said as two figures stepped from the shadows nearby and into the full moonlight. "We were expecting your husband, not you."

"Come on, Copper Jack. You've seen a Scottish kilt in your lifetime," Bustle replied. "Not only is it an honor to wear into battle, for what the three of us need to accomplish tonight, I need the freedom of movement."

"Like every American, I have always wondered what exactly exists underneath a Scottish kilt anyway," Smitty joked. Bustle refused to take the bait, eager to cut short the silly banter and get on with the serious business at hand.

"If you must know, Yank, you'll find a brave Scotsman under every Scottish kilt and tonight you're going to get a bird's eye view from the bottom. Just hope your back is up to the task."

Bustle motioned for Smitty to assume a crouching position to make it easier for Copper to mount Smitty's shoulder blades. Smitty was pleasantly surprised to find Copper not as heavy as he imagined. Once Copper's feet were firmly balanced on Smitty's shoulders, Smitty cupped his hands together to give Bustle the toe-hold he needed to scale the full height of both his partners in crime. As the full weight of Bustle settled in on both of them, Copper shouted his encouragement to his fellow anchorman below. "Smitty, just like raising the stars and stripes at Iwo Jima, don't you think?"

Once Bustle was safely positioned on top of Copper Jack, Smitty tried to ignore the burning sensation in his shoulders and slowly stood upright, as did Copper Jack, allowing the human chain to reach its full height. Eventually, Bustle stared eyeball-to-eyeball at the statue of the Portuguese king. Unfortunately, when Bustle reached for the king's crown, it was rusted into place and would require some coaxing.

While Bustle wrestled to free the crown, Captain Baptiste took a pensive step forward out of the shadows. Drunken Brits were certainly not uncommon at that hour of the night. However, the good Captain could not quite believe the melodrama unfolding before his very eyes and removed the revolver from his holster as a precaution.

At the very moment the crown was finally wrenched loose, Bustle placed the crown squarely on his own head and turned immediately philosophic. Under the light of a full moon and the steady effects of the alcohol he had consumed, Bustle took time to mourn the loss of his wife's fidelity with Virgo and felt compelled to recite a few bittersweet lines from the poet, Robert Burns:

"Had we never lov'd sae kindly
Had we never lov'd sae blindly
Never met – or never parted
We had ne'er been broken hearted."

Copper was suddenly beside himself with anger. "Bustle, have you gone completely crackers? Smitty, get us down from here, for Christ sakes!" Suddenly, an unintended warning shot from the pistol of Captain Baptiste whistled just above their heads, echoing through the village square like a pinball bursting in the eardrums of the three saboteurs. Under his tartan kilt, Bilkington released an unintended shot of his own, urinating on the startled Copper Jack and Smitty before they all collapsed in a heap at the foot of the statue.

As if Bustle losing control of his kidneys was not enough to cope with, Captain Baptiste suddenly stepped forward from the shadows and showered them with verbal abuse. They didn't need a translator to realize they were in big trouble. Turns out the gun of Captain Baptiste had discharged accidentally, so he was as startled and upset as they were. Copper and Smitty scrambled to their feet as best they could. Bustle, who had taken the longest fall, was still flat on his back. The Captain checked their passports by flashlight and recognized the photo of Copper Jack immediately.

"Senor Zack?" he asked.

"Bom Dia," was all Copper could think to say.

"Si. Bom Dia," the Captain agreed, checking is wristwatch with the flashlight, annoyed that he should be off duty at this hour of the day instead of babysitting a bunch of drunken Brits. Copper removed the crown from Bustle's weary head, returned it dutifully to the hands of Captain Baptiste, and then opened up his wallet. They shook hands.

"Obrigado," the Captain said, tipping his hat before leaving.

"That's it?" Smitty asked. "We're free to go? What did you do, Copper Jack?"

"Reminded him he owed me a favor," Copper said, returning his wallet to his pocket.

At last Casa Bodega was a ghost of its former self. All the dinner guests had paired up and left for the evening. As predicted, the Portuguese singer, Jose, became King of Persia for one fateful night. His fellow guitarist surrendered to the advances of runner-up, Mrs Yorkshire. Mrs Chippendale escorted one of the lucky Portuguese winos up the street to her marble staircase on Millionaire Hill and Frill Pimpton invited to her home the other lucky wino. The fado had been kind to everyone but the bartender. Copper Jack arrived at the bodega to find Liz all alone, sitting on her orange crate behind the bar, downing double whiskies between the refrain: "One for me ... and one for my baby."

"I brought you some company, Liz," Copper announced. Bilkington Bustle drooped lifelessly over Copper's left shoulder.

"I don't believe it. I must be completely sloshed," Liz insisted. "Last time I saw you, I thought it was Tookie you carted around unceremoniously. What am I supposed to do with Bustle?" she demanded.

"As you can see, he's had a rough night. It would be better if he slept it off here at the bodega, if you have a spare room. No reason to disturb Mrs Bustle at this unseemly hour of the night."

"And the crown?"

"Safe for now. I tipped off my good friend, Captain Baptiste. Invited him to join our little tea-party in the roundabout just to make sure nothing got out of hand."

"And the Yank?"

"In my car. If you agree to take on Bustle, I'll let the Yank sleep it off at my place."

"So, how did you suddenly become guardian angel to Bustle and Smitty when I've been waiting patiently for you all my life?"

"It's been quite a day," Copper admitted, without answering her question. "Protected my wife's reputation, saved the necks of Smitty and Bustle and returned the king's crown to the Portuguese authorities. Suppose there is a special place in heaven for former ambulance drivers still doing good deeds?" he asked.

"Not unless you also manage to save me from myself."

"I brought you a roommate instead. Where do you want the body, Liz? I've been lifting Bustle up all evening and he's not getting any lighter."

"Put him in Smitty's room for the night, if you must. It's the only bed left." Copper followed Liz up the stairway to Smitty's room and literally dropped Bustle into bed with a thud. While Liz tucked Bustle under the sheets, Scottish kilt and all, Copper couldn't help skimming over a few sentences from a page in Smitty's typewriter.

"Sure you won't stay?" Liz asked. Copper looked up from the typewriter and reminded Liz there were no more beds left in the bodega. "Just one, the only bed the matters, mine." Copper was on his way down the stairway before he would have to answer the question. Liz ran after him. "One more question before you leave. Why are you really kidnapping the Yank tonight?" Copper reluctantly paused at the foot of the stairway and waited for Liz to catch up.

"Remember that chat we had earlier this evening about growing old?"

"Yes, and look how much we've aged just since the conversation," she nodded.

"I've decided time is running out for me. I need to somehow pass the baton, share my small legacy with someone young enough and wise enough to benefit, or everything will be lost."

"You're going to ask Smitty to write about your life, aren't you?"

"Liz, if Smitty doesn't realize why he arrived on Copper Jack's doorstep one day, I do know why. Things like this happen for a reason."

"And will your book mention me, Copper Jack?" Liz asked, feeling suddenly faint before falling at his feet all together. After lifting her body up gallantly and escorting her safely to her bedroom, Copper asked the obvious question.

"Be honest, Liz. Did you fake the dizzy spell just to get me into your bedroom," he asked, resting her body carefully across the bed.

"Looks like it worked, doesn't it?" she whispered, opening her eyes and smiling back at him in the light of the full moon. Copper tried to excuse himself politely, but Liz held onto him tightly. "At least lie next to me on top of the blanket in your civvies, if you won't join me under the sheets. Just until I fall asleep," she begged.

The bed was intimate. The old mattress sank miserably at the middle and curled up along the sides, throwing them together with only a coverlet separating their bodies. Liz buried her nose in Copper's chest, found his sternum warm and stayed there. Copper waited until she dozed off before he left Casa Bodega once and for all.

7

A Part of the Sun Never Rises

His eyesight was no longer postcard clear, so Copper Jack squinted under the yellow light and forced himself to hold the paperback book at arm's length. Can't submit to the ravages of old age just yet, he decided, because there was still too much work to be done. He turned the pages of the dog-eared detective story quickly. The cardboard characters were trapped in a fast-paced plot, and it mattered not who was being followed, raped or shot at as long as the detective always came out on top in the end. This was the literature of choice among Brits in the Algarve.

If the genre didn't exactly expand the mind, at least it kept pumping blood to the brain cells. Most books passed from hand to hand so frequently their pages finally faded over time and were often dog-eared in the corners, pages barely bound precariously to a cracked and broken spine and because of the handling by so many sweaty palms, the books usually reeked like the musty armpits of an old overcoat, adding dimension for which the seedy storyline no doubt benefited.

"Well, yes, I guess we'll see about that," Copper murmured to himself, content he was always a step ahead of the antagonist. Yet each time Copper turned another page, like the protagonist, he was blind-sided in the same dark alley, by the same gush of over confidence. In the end it didn't really matter because the detective always emerged immortal.

Soon Smitty emerged unsteadily from the shadows of a nearby guestroom to join Copper in the parlor. Smitty blinked his eyes repeatedly, nursing a robust hangover. "I've been waylaid," Smitty said, addressing his complaint toward Copper and his armchair.

"Tied one on, did you?" Copper smiled.

"And buried the corpse, I'm afraid," Smitty confessed.

"Then what are you doing on your feet staggering around my parlor before sunrise?"

"I should ask you the same question. You had as much to drink as I did."

"I'm always awake this time of day, Smitty. Truth is, old people don't really sleep because they're afraid they may not wake up. Here, let me make you a cup of my favorite breakfast concoction. It will help you thaw out a bit."

"Or pick up where I left off," Smitty worried, as he watched Copper pour two jiggers of brandy and a teaspoon of sugar into a cup of boiling water. After blowing on the drink to cool it down a bit, Smitty sipped slowly and methodically, until his head began to crawl out of the fog. Events from the previous evening were still hazy.

"So whatever happened to Bustle—I mean, after he emptied his bladder all over us?" Smitty suddenly recalled.

"Dropped him off in your bed in the bodega."

"So if Bustle's sleeping it off at Casa Bodega, what am I doing here?" Smitty asked.

"You've been kidnapped, by me. I'll explain why later. But first, drink up," Copper recommended, pouring Smitty another brandy. Copper glanced at his wristwatch, noticed the time of day and set aside his paperback book for later. He clicked on the trusty wireless at his side and assumed a solemn position in his armchair. He lit another cigarette and gave a final stir to the sugar in his cup, which had settled to the bottom of his brandy like the grains of an hourglass.

"This is the British Broadcasting Company," the news cast began.

Smitty soon nodded off to sleep on the couch and Copper was left to endure the radio broadcast alone. It didn't take him long, however, to get disgusted with the news he heard and shut off the wireless in a fit of anger. As he always did after digesting the troubling headlines of the day, it was time to vent his spleen, whether Smitty wanted to hear it or not.

"Thousands unemployed, striking, starving and rioting in the streets, and thousands more overcrowding our hospitals and prisons, not to mention thousands suffering in our nursing homes because our lame government laws won't permit them to switch off no matter how much pain they have to endure." In mid-sentence, Smitty returned to semi-consciousness again, not yet fully awake enough to appreciate the sweep and scope of Copper's world view.

"Here's one of the great many stupidities of modern civilization, Smitty. A man does not have the right to determine the circumstances of his own death. Some of us are lucky enough to die painlessly, slumped over in our flower-garden in full bloom. Yet too many old people are asked to carry on long after their bodies give out, or to live totally destitute with cardboard lining their shoes and newspaper filling the sleeves of their jackets just trying to stay warm."

Begrudgingly, Smitty finally made himself sit more upright and pay more attention in the face of the sober realities spewing forth from Copper's fire hose. "Talk about the lunacy of government's law against suicide. How do you prosecute a dead man? And let's not overlook the complicity of the Church, which won't admit any of us into the green, green pastures of afterlife if we die by our own hand. So our laws, our morality and our miracle drugs keep our bodies hanging on by a thread long after our minds have closed up shop." There was such finality to everything Copper Jack said, it made it difficult to refute his ideas, Smitty decided, so he listened intently and swallowed hard in silence.

"Let me give you a personal example. I know an old couple in England, known them since childhood. Their children are grown and gone, living their own lives and don't really want to be bothered with their parents anymore. Most of this couple's friends have died or moved away. So, whenever I'm in England I always pay them a visit because I know they don't get many visitors anymore.

"The old man always offers me his armchair, which I refuse politely, because I know in his lifetime no one ever sits in that chair except him. Anyway, we go back and forth until I give in and sit in his chair next to his wife as he pulls up a stool between us. The three of us reminisce for hours and have a wonderful time. Even at sixty years old, I'm like a son to them and I know when it's time for me to leave. The two of them will still be talking about our reunion a couple of days later like it's the highlight of their lives." Copper paused for a moment, took a draw from his cigarette and a sip of brandy, stared across at Smitty until he was sure the young American was following his story, if not his logic. To show his attention never wavered, Smitty moved to the edge of the sofa, leaned forward with his elbows on his knees and cupped his hands beneath his chin.

"They each suffer arthritis and the usual annoying ailments of old age but the deepest pain comes from loneliness. I can see the emptiness in their eyes. They sit each side of the fireplace all day, like you and I are doing here, but share very little conversation anymore. After all those years together, what's left to say, other than to repeat yourself all over again? The missus might say suddenly: 'Dear, isn't it about time to throw another log on?' because staying warm is their only real need anymore. He will throw a log on the fire and they will watch it burn down together. That's the full extent of their final days together. Each day becomes a little more painful and lonelier than the previous. Every minute they lose a little more dignity."

Smitty leaned back into the sofa and knocked off his brandy to brace himself for the inevitable end of the narrative. At this point in his story, Copper stared off into space as if a full audience was waiting to be enlightened, living and dying on his every word. "Two loving people, deeply religious and law-abiding citizens, ought to be able to look one another in the eye when the day has come and ask, 'Do you think it's time, sweetheart?' And if they agree, they should be able to notify the authorities of their decision to switch off. What could be more sensible or humane? A man and woman, having lived a good life together, should be able to decide to pack it in together. Not in some macabre suicide pact which is how you read about it in the newspapers, I'm talking about a legally and medically supervised decision, with the good graces of Church and family members. As it stands now, unfortunately, most old people are just trapped inside their own bodies counting down the time."

Copper looked back at Smitty again, embarrassed suddenly. He had dominated the conversation like an old wind bag. To break the mood, if only for a moment, Copper smiled slyly and asked, "Should I throw another log on?" Smitty only nodded without speaking because it was clear Copper was not yet ready to yield the floor.

"I just don't want to count down the time," Copper said, making good on his promise to throw another log on the fire. "Want my time to count for something. I know I should be grateful for my little plot of land in the Algarve where I may yet die peacefully in my flower garden. Yet when I hear the outrages over the wireless every morning, I want to run back to the UK and do something about it.

"Of course at my age, what could I possibly do that would matter? Become a Hyde Park derelict, frequent Speaker's Corner and answer my own rants? Tookie says I already do that here in our sitting room, anyway. I just don't want to become another hapless old fool afraid of his own shadow." As Copper's voice trailed off, he squinted toward Smitty through a thick cloud of cigarette smoke. In the aftermath of his latest soliloquy, Copper felt obliged to pay Smitty a long overdue compliment.

"You're a good listener, Yank."

"Probably haven't sobered up yet."

"No, don't sell yourself short. Writers listen because they know we have two ears and only one mouth for a reason. That's why I kidnapped you last night. I've decided an old man with something to say needs a young man willing to learn and to write about it. Don't know what brought you to Portugal, Smitty, doesn't really matter anymore. We will both know the reason soon enough if you get the book written."

Copper paused long enough to sip his brandy and to light another cigarette, and long enough for Smitty to recall Virgo's prophecy about him meeting someone important. "I have a few pounds stored away Tookie doesn't know about, not a lot of money mind you, so you will be paid for your work. I figure we'll need a few more sessions like the one this morning, if you can suffer an old fool his last wish. Won't ask to see what you write, only want to know you're listening. I'm full up with things to get off my chest before I go. You decide if my life is worth more than a sow's tail to anyone else but me. I think I've lived a book. See if you can write it. What do you say, Yank?"

This time it was Copper who leaned forward in his chair anticipating the answer, while Smitty said nothing. At first blush, the surprise proposal didn't exactly grab him by the lapels. So how do you turn down politely an honest man's final request Smitty wondered?

"I'll think about it," Smitty surrendered.

"Think about it," Copper agreed, "but not too long."

He was snoring effortlessly under a heap of warm blankets when Virgo slipped quietly inside his room. She pulled back the drapes from the window to let in the bright sunshine, just enough light on the subject to expose her shapely figure beneath the sheer camisole, and enough daylight in the room for her to read a lonely page left behind in Smitty's typewriter:

"He had experienced many women since, several of them beautiful and provocative in their own way. He had written many stories about these experiences, except not about the first one. For him, the first love had always been the last and most difficult to understand. He knew the countless romances that followed were foolish attempts to recapture the first. And yet, here he was at the typewriter once again, trying to reclaim the feelings in words that he could never adequately express when he held her tightly in his arms."

Suddenly, Virgo was interrupted from her reading by a scratchy voice coming from the bed. "I feel like hell. But seeing you here, surely I have died and gone to heaven," exclaimed Bilkington Bustle, propping up his heavy head on one elbow, admiring Virgo's youthful looking flesh across the room.

"Bilkington!" she shouted with surprise.

"At your service, of course."

"What in hell are you doing in Smitty's room?"

"I could ask you the same question, couldn't I? Just let me get my bearings for a moment. It's all starting to come back to me," he said, resting his throbbing head back down on the pillow. "Last thing I remember was that blasted gunshot scaring the pee out of me. In fact, it's still ringing in my ears."

"Gunshot? Who? Why?" she panicked, thinking of Smitty's safety.

"Not sure, because after the gunshot someone pulled the rug right out from under me. Been unconscious ever since, that is, until you decided to tiptoe into my room. Please tell me I'm not dreaming."

"Obviously, I was looking for Smitty – not you," she said, edging closer to the door.

"No need to rush off," Bustle insisted, jumping to his feet to block her path. "What counts in life is how we play the cards we've been dealt. And quite frankly, I very much like the cards I'm holding at the moment," he said smiling, as he placed his hand on her bare shoulder and slipped off the strap of her camisole to reveal one of her voluptuous breasts.

"Bugger off, Bustle," she demanded, jerking free from his grasp. "Something especially rank about a man dressed in drag," she said, staring down scornfully at the knobby knees in full view beneath his tartan kilt.

"Don't get huffy with me. Chasing skirts is exactly your cup of tea. Mrs Bustle told me all about it."

"You're bluffing, Bustle, as always. Out of my way now," she ordered, although Bustle refused to step aside.

"You may have your way with the women, Virgo, but not the men. At least not, this man, not after what you did to the missus."

"She had the time of her life," Virgo taunted him.

"Then so will I," he promised, grabbing Virgo by both shoulders and forcing her down onto the bed. Bustle held Virgo's wrists with one hand and unsnapped the bottom of her camisole with his free hand. In one quick motion, he hiked up the kilt around his waist and lowered himself on top of her. However, unlike the fantasy where he filled Virgo with every ounce of sexual venom he could muster, in real life Bustle went flaccid. Couldn't get it up enough to part two rose petals in the garden, let alone penetrate a pair of thighs poised against him. As his hold on Virgo weakened, she pushed him off the side of the bed and left him grumbling to himself in the floor, a lame duck rapist.

"Now you know why I do what I do, because you can't. You should thank me for keeping all your women happy," she said, escaping out of the door without waiting for his gratitude.

Downstairs at the bodega, Liz was grinning to herself behind the bar like a Cheshire cat. The fado the night before had filled the till. The reverend was due back in town and, thanks to Copper Jack's thoughtfulness, she had enjoyed a good night's sleep. Even the sudden presence of Bilkington Bustle at the bar couldn't rain on her parade.

"OK, Liz. How much do I owe you for the room last night?" he asked, embarrassed to be there at all.

"Nothing, it's on the house as a favor to Copper Jack."

"I should have known. He also must be the one who stole my crown."

"Bustle, you old fool, you came in here last night passed out wearing nothing on your head but a large hangover. Copper Jack had the good sense to tip off Captain Baptiste in advance of your plan. So you owe Copper your thanks for keeping you out of the clinker for drunken and disorderly conduct."

"I should have known," Bustle said, sounding thoroughly disgusted, "undone by our meddlesome philanthropist, sage and father figure of the Algarve. He has gone too far this time. I shall pay Copper a visit he will never forget."

"You might want to check in with Mrs Bustle first, since she spent another night alone."

"So did I," Bustle said without remorse, shoving his way through the fortress doors and outside into the painful light of day.

Mrs Bustle perched outside on her bedroom balcony as she did most days, except today would be different. With her prized binoculars, she surveyed the whole of the Algarve for the last time.

Beneath a cloud-spattered sky of crude finger paint, Portuguese women sleepwalk to market and seem startled when their windblown shawls dance mystically about the neck and shoulders. Retired fishermen squat at outside cafes, laughing and fussing with their caps and shirt collars. Thin-blooded hounds roam the town and rouse the energy to chase after the teasing gusts of wind. Mules feel whips against their backsides as two-wheeled carts hasten along cobblestone streets with a sense of urgency.

In winter, sidewalk markets move indoors where vegetables taste musty. Trees shed leaves. Beaches lose shoreline. Rain-clouds scurry across the sky, burst, and somehow leave behind no puddles and, in winter, church bells sound more distant, muffled, apologetic to the ear – along this coast of inlet bays and outlet qualms, a community singed with the winds of recrimination.

Eventually her binoculars focused on the statue of the Portuguese king. His crown was missing so Mrs Bustle forced a smile. Mission accomplished and no doubt Bilkington celebrated his success by toasting away the night in the arms of another woman. She did not leave behind a personal note, just the family photo album sitting on her bed open to some of her favorite images, her eternal protest against time passing and changing the way things were once upon a time. When she finally found the courage to jump from the balcony, Mrs Bustle fell silently in flight without even a peep, the last bird to fly south for the winter. Her neck snapped like a dry twig when her body met the earth beneath her.

When Smitty finally left Copper Jack's villa, the silver Citroen was waiting eagerly for him by the curb. "Need a lift back to the bodega?" Virgo asked. Smitty rested his forearms against the car and peered in through the open window at Virgo's delightful tennis skirt and her chubby thighs hugging the leather upholstery like adhesive.

"I'll take you up on the offer. I'm getting used to being abducted."

"We need to talk," was all she said.

On the drive back to Casa Bodega, Virgo described for Smitty her recent misadventures with Bustle. They were both laughing out loud by the end of her story.

"I had my own doubts about the legitimacy of Bustle's kilt," Smitty admitted.

"By the way, I owe you an apology," Virgo confessed.

"I can't imagine why?"

"When I was in your room with Bustle, I read the page you left behind in your typewriter. From what I read, I assume you were writing about yourself."

"That's what most writers do, don't you think?"

"Then I had it right all along. You are running away from another woman."

"Or, perhaps, just trying to escape the memory of her."

"Then I guess I don't understand after all," Virgo said.

"That's exactly why I have to write about her, to finally understand," Smitty admitted.

"But you have not been writing lately."

"I will write again soon. I have just been commissioned." Smitty had made his decision. He would put on hold the story of his long-lost love in the days ahead until he could explore more fully Copper's mind and Virgo's body.

Copper didn't pull any punches. "Bustle, I notice you have been calling at my villa frequently since my accident. Should I attribute this to concern about my health? Or is it more like a vulture hovering over the carcass and the woman who will survive me?"

"I would like to think I've used more discretion than that, Copper Jack," Bustle suggested.

"Yes, that's right, you're about as subtle as the clap between your legs."

"OK, then. If that's where the conversation's going, I have a firm proposition for you, deadly serious."

"Spare me the details, Bustle. I would rather take my medicine directly and hear the bad news firsthand from my wife."

"Unfortunately, you are a picture of health again, Copper. Well on the road to recovery, much to my chagrin. Without the help of Mother Nature, I have no choice but to take matters into my own hands. No use pretending there is any love lost between us. And you are right, of course, I am very fond of Tookie. So, I'm no longer willing to wait for you to bugger off. I challenge you to a duel."

"A what?" Copper asked, sounding dumfounded.

"A duel, you know, the gentlemen's way of sorting out their differences."

"You mean as in ten paces, turn and fire?"

"As long as both of us can be trusted not to stop counting at nine."

"Is this another of your silly pranks, Bustle?"

"On the contrary, old chap. As I said, I'm deadly serious. And we must tell no one, especially your comrade, Captain Baptiste. To avoid potential outside interference, we shall stage the event this spring on the deck of my yacht, when the weather's good and the deck's steady: just you, me and the ocean, and far enough from shore to avoid the authorities. When it's over, the survivor can throw the body overboard to the sharks, no questions asked. What do you say, Copper Jack?"

"You know you will never get her from me without a fight."

Before Bustle could respond, Tookie suddenly walked into the parlor, interrupted their discussion and invited Bustle to stay for lunch. Having achieved what he came to accomplish, Bustle politely took a rain check on her offer.

"Thanks, but I should get back home before the missus starts to worry. I was just telling Copper we should all shove off this spring aboard my yacht. Take a holiday."

Copper Jack would survive another winter, then.

8

Last Land of Hope and Glory

Springtime came with a bang.

By choice, Copper Jack had not fired a gun since the war. Now he had no choice. He squeezed the trigger slowly as his life whizzed by in a blur of memories, some good, some not so good. It ended with a single blast from the hand gun. He blinked, smelled smoke from the barrel and felt very glad to be alive.

Sometimes it required the simple act of firing a hand gun to remind a man he was still a force to be reckoned with, even if his errant shot missed its target just ten paces away. Copper made several practice pivots before firing the pistol again, as if his pivot was at fault and not his aim. Even without the pivot, standing motionless at point blank range, the target seemed to shift. Lately shapes would come and go in his field of vision. Mostly, it was Copper's eyesight that was coming and going.

He complained to no one, not even himself. He practiced alone in an open field on an early spring day. The morning air felt cool against the sweat beads forming on his bare chest. When he was reasonably confident he had finally mastered the pivot move, he began firing a shot after each quick spin. Yet shot after shot disappeared into the dawn without leaving a single mark on the target, Copper's undershirt, pinned to the trunk of a nearby tree. Worse yet, the undershirt waved mockingly back and forth in the breeze like the white flag of surrender. The best Copper could do was stare holes in his makeshift target.

Finally, Copper turned his back on the target and shrugged his shoulders in half-resignation. If he hoped to have one lucky shot left in him, he decided, why waste it in practice anyway? Yet he knew he was kidding himself. He simply had to get better. So he turned to face the target once more, steadied his shooting hand with his off hand, squinting hard as he tried to sort the shapes from their shadows. He fired the next shot as if his life depended on it. A branch snapped and fell from the tree, a worse shot than all the rest. The undershirt waved in the breeze apparently untouched.

Copper's body began to chill, so he retrieved his undershirt as his legs gave out and he sat at the base of the tree trying to collect his wits. With his back resting against the trunk of the tree, he stared off into what was now a bright, fiery horizon. His mind wandered. To save his life he could not remember how many practice shots he fired, but it would only take one shot to make things right. He decided he would never give Bustle the satisfaction.

To raise the pistol to his head required both hands because they were shaking noticeably. To pull the trigger on himself demanded a silent prayer, even for an atheist. Only when he bowed his head to pray, with the gun barrel resting flush against his temple, did he notice the hole in his undershirt, a bullet hole, just above the heart. Copper whirled around to inspect the tree trunk where the bullet entered. Sure enough, one of his practice shots hit the mark after all, a small glimmer of hope. One accurate shot was all a duel required.

"Copper Jack, where have you been all morning long?" Tookie asked when he returned home. "We are at war."

"Then maybe you and I should call a truce."

"Not you and me, England's at war," she corrected him, standing nervously beside the wireless and straining to hear every word of the broadcast. "Bloody Argentina," Tookie said finally, turning up the volume.

The dead weight of Copper Jack fell back into his armchair as the BBC broadcast confirmed the impossible: Argentina had forcibly taken over the Falkland Islands, one of the last remaining outposts of the British Empire. Tookie steadied a world map in Copper's lap, pointing to the tiny speck of islands off the coast of Argentina, an area no bigger than Wales and eight thousand miles from the UK. "We've been humiliated," she announced.

"A few rocks in the middle of the ocean thousands of miles from nowhere," Copper muttered, shaking his head in despair.

For the next several weeks, the Algarve was in a complete tizzy; rejuvenated might be a better word. Maggie Thatcher endeared herself to all Englishmen by dispatching the Fleet to the South Atlantic without flinching. After all, Britain once ruled the high seas as it had ruled the world.

The Algarve experienced a sudden revival of English bluster and tradition. Women would 'lie back and think of England' during intercourse. The Union Jack was raised proudly from the masts of every villa and pub in town. A civilian militia was formed, presumably to keep a watchful eye on Portugal's coastline to see if sympathizers from Spain would be foolish enough to unleash the Armada to try and intercept the British Fleet. On both sides of the war, there was no end to the absurdities fanned by the fervor of overzealous patriotism.

Bilkington Bustle, for example, announced suddenly he was setting sail in his yacht to join the Fleet en-route to Argentina. "Even the 'Queen Elizabeth' has been requisitioned," Bustle explained. "Every boat available mates. We are at war. If the Fleet won't have me, I'll go it alone."

Of course, such a display of bravado called for a proper public send off. A rally was hosted at Casa Bodega in honor of Bustle and all the brave young lads of the UK who were shipping out from Portsmouth. At home and abroad, pomp and circumstance became the new order of the day.

Reverend Pat faced a full congregation for the first time since his eulogy at the funeral services of Mrs Bustle. The funeral had been a macabre event. Efforts to straighten Mrs Bustle's broken neck had failed miserably. For those paying their last respects, the contorted neck looking up from the casket was an ugly reminder of the grim circumstances surrounding her death.

Officially, it had been ruled an accident, but whispers of suicide persisted throughout the community. Some believed Bilkington Bustle was coping far better than he should, so soon after his wife's untimely death. The outbreak of the Falklands War was just the diversion everyone needed. The war would serve an even higher purpose, at least according to Reverend Pat's sermon. "Only last winter we gathered here in God's house to celebrate the anniversary of the Battle of Britain, although we know from history it was not Britain's battle alone. It was a key battle in the war to end all wars, a war fought so our children, and the children of all free people, would never know such ravages and devastation in their lifetime. With God's blessings, peace has triumphed ever since, until now. That is why our beloved Britannia must prevail again as she sets sail to do battle in the unfriendly waters of the South Atlantic."

The congregation could tell from the outset, Reverend Pat was in rare form. By the time he reached his emotional conclusion, the congregation was certain beyond any shadow of a doubt that the God who looked down from heaven was lily white, took tea and spoke with a British accent. "I know even the most patriotic among us have grave reservations about such a confrontation, concerns shared by all peace-loving, God-fearing people. And yet, how can we in good conscience turn our backs on an open act of aggression by a fascist country, a country infamous for crimes against its own people? Surely citizens of the free world would be the next to suffer.

"Therefore, let us set aside our faint-hearted reservations. Let us withhold criticism of our leaders who must guide our Fleet to victory. Let us wish them God's speed in reclaiming the peace. Let us praise the Land of Hope and Glory; and let us pray."

After prayers and hymns and a few thunderous rounds of "God Save the Queen," the congregation was more than ready for several rounds of gin and tonic at the bar. Bustle concluded an emotional testimonial with a vindictive toast: "Up your junta, Argies!"

Frill Pimpton toasted Bustle's journey by giving him something to look forward to upon his return. To the delight of everyone, she removed her blouse and bra and bared her breasts to the world, exposing a fresh tattoo above each boob, the letter 'U' above the left and the letter 'K' above the right.

After the crowd left the bodega, they reconvened the rally down by the waterfront where Bustle would board his yacht with pride, cheered by the familiar cry of bagpipes blaring and voices singing 'Auld Lang Syne'. His yacht, the HMS Victory, was named after Captain Nelson's ship, which proved victorious at the Battle of Trafalgar in the 19th century. Unlike Captain Nelson, however, Bustle would lead an all-Portuguese crew of hired mercenaries into battle, more likely retired fishermen bored with their wives and looking for adventure.

Bustle also managed to acquire an old hand-me-down cannon resurrected from a salvage yard nearby. He figured the cannon would protect his yacht's broadside, although the chap at the salvage yard who sold it to him warned the gun was likely to misfire. Before boarding his yacht and shoving off to parts unknown, Bustle paid Tookie an intimate farewell. "Keep a candle in the window, Tookie, as a beacon to guide me home," Bustle ordered.

"Don't come a cropper, Bilkington," she said tearfully.

"Can't be as bad as Northern Ireland, now can it? By the way, please relay this message to Copper: feuds between nations supersede feuds over women. He will understand what I mean. Cheerio, then."

Bustle doffed his brightly plumed hat repeatedly to his well-wishers as the yacht took its own sweet time steering clear of the harbor and striking out for open seas. Beneath sun-drenched parasols and colorful cabanas, the loyal gathering waved back at him admiringly with white hankies until the boat was out of sight. What bolstered Bustle's spirits the most though, was a last glimpse of Frill's naked breasts, which through his binoculars looked like a pair of distant cannons pointed pertly toward the enemy.

"Well, Smitty, there you have it," Copper said, pointing an accusing finger at the wireless. "The British Fleet is sailing forth like drunks staggering bleary-eyed out of a pub caught fire. It is a dark day for Britain and for some reason, everyone's making merry."

Once again, Copper Jack found himself on the other side of the fence from the rest of the world. He refused to leave his vigil beside the wireless since the first report of conflict, and over time his armchair came to look like a Field Marshal's outpost. He had not shaved, changed underwear or emptied the ashtray, which was finally overflowing onto the floor at his feet. On the map in his lap he had reluctantly plotted the likely course of the Fleet across the Atlantic, still hoping to hear some distant and reassuring voice over the wireless, like a Churchill or a Roosevelt, to make some sense of the blood that would spill.

"If Argentina fired first, well then, we must go in. We have always protected our own at any cost anywhere in the world, and we must do it properly, not like your Vietnam muck-up. However, mark my words, Smitty, history will show the fault came long before the first shot was fired." Out of frustration, Copper tossed the map to the floor near the cigarette ashes. Out of the corner of his eye, Smitty paid careful attention to make sure a live ember didn't light up the map and the entire parlor in flames.

"*Labourites* can't hang the albatross on Thatcher. Ordering the Fleet into action was the will of the people but the Foreign Office, the *Ministry of Defence* and Parliament all have blood on their hands and have failed our Prime Minister severely in the area of diplomacy. Worst of all, they have failed our young men, many of whom will be shipped home in body-bags before it's over, if we're lucky enough to find their bodies. Look at the expanse of ocean in that part of the world," Copper insisted, retrieving the map again to help punctuate his geography lesson. Smitty shook his head in disbelief.

"I know how fickle the sea can be, Smitty. The last time they fished me out of the English Channel, my teeth had been chattering for forty-eight hours. It was probably the only thing that kept my heart pumping. The rest of my body was numb for days after. I still feel the cold in my bones from time to time."

Copper's mind flashed again on the insanity of his upcoming duel with Bustle. His eyesight was not his only handicap. Copper wondered why he agreed to duel Bustle on his yacht when he had developed a mortal fear of water ever since his war experiences.

"We will lose men to the sea no matter how poorly the Argentines shoot. Don't take me for a traitor, Smitty, I still love my country above all else."

Up to this point, Smitty's interviews with Copper had all been one-sided: Copper only talking about subjects of his interest and largely ignoring the aspects of his life Smitty always wanted to probe. Besides forgivable lapses of memory, Copper insisted on expressing his opinions about the state of the world rather than focus on his own life lessons. When it was obvious the interviews were going nowhere, Smitty gave Copper a tape recorder and suggested Copper try dictating his most private thoughts into the machine whenever he was alone. Copper bristled at the thought. "Tried that, didn't I. But whenever I hit the replay button, it didn't sound like my voice or my life," he explained in frustration.

The bitter truth was that Copper had become disenchanted with the smallness of his life when put under the microscope. He had mistakenly associated the noble ideas his mind generated in abundance, with noble deeds and actions, of which there were very few he could point to other than his war experiences. Tookie had been correct all along, he decided. He really had not achieved anything noteworthy in his life. Ironically, a cornerstone of Copper's personal philosophy was to live as free of regrets as possible, but as he neared the finish line, the regrets were starting to pile up like dirty laundry in the corner demanding a long rinse cycle. Suddenly, Copper broke his own silence. "Can I ask you a personal question, Smitty? Might sound daft coming from an old dinosaur like me, but have you ever completely lost your mind over a woman?"

Smitty did not hesitate. "Only once but never again."

"Probably just as well," Copper agreed. "I've seen grown men willing to kill for love, or be killed," he said, swallowing hard. Lately, Smitty noticed the subject of death came up with increasing frequency with Copper. More than a morose preoccupation, the discussion usually revolved around getting his house in order and becoming more reflective than he had been in the past. "Will you be returning to the States when this is over?" Copper asked. Smitty nodded. "Back to the woman you once loved?" Copper probed.

"That would be difficult for lots of reasons."

"Might she be worth all the trouble?"

"Once upon a time..." Smitty didn't bother to finish the thought because they were interrupted by another news bulletin on the Falklands War, an increasing preoccupation with Copper Jack these days. When the news update was over, Copper resumed his train of thought.

"I have a confession, Smitty. I'm about to get myself killed over a woman." With Smitty leaning forward intently, Copper went on to explain the circumstances of his upcoming duel with Bustle. "I'm only telling you this because you are writing my story. Obviously, it's not for the world to know until after I'm gone, rather if I'm gone," he corrected himself quickly.

Motivation for the duel was more difficult for him to articulate, however. "It seems the closer I come to signing off, and I've had my share of near misses in my lifetime, the more I still want to live. Maybe that's what war does to you. I appreciate life more today than when I was a young buck trying to throw it all away on some forgotten battlefield. Strange as this may sound, Smitty, the worse my eyesight becomes, the better I see things more clearly than before. Unfortunately, this sudden desire to go on living makes me timid at a time when I most need my courage."

The irony of Tookie Jack's sudden arrival at that precise moment, still flush in the face and teary-eyed from Bustle's farewell at sea, was not lost on Smitty. He realized he had already learned more about Copper from what he didn't say and from the people close to him, than he would ever hear directly from the horse's mouth.

"Well, it's done, then," Tookie announced, sounding befuddled and standing in the middle of parlor, not knowing what to do next. "Bilkington's off to sea after all. Sure hope your United States gets off the fence, Yank, and pitches in on this war." Only then did Tookie address Copper for the first time, relaying Bustle's coded message.

Rather than sounding relieved that the duel would be postponed, Copper merely scoffed. "Bustle's yacht will be fired upon by a few sea gulls and he'll return home immediately to put in for a Distinguished Service Cross," Copper predicted.

"At least he's doing something," Tookie retaliated.

"So why didn't you go with him?" Copper asked.

"Why didn't you? You were the ship's gunner, or so you tell us over and over again." Copper squinted his eyes in anger and peered back at Tookie with a piercing look.

"I did my bit in a real war, having to kill teenagers in the end. At their age I was still sneaking in the back door of the village cinema to catch the latest Errol Flynn movie. So, don't talk to me about war, woman, lost my stomach for it long ago."

After she stormed out of the room, Copper broke the awkward silence. "So that's the woman I'm fighting for, Smitty. You must think I'm crackers. Believe it or not, we really are quite fond of one another. But don't turn your head," he smiled finally, "or you'll miss it."

Back at Casa Bodega, Smitty gazed listlessly out of the open window of his room and gave in to the intoxication that comes from surviving winter in a foreign land and waking one day to find spring. This was a land where life could be simple, such as the scene unfolding in the village street below.

The Portuguese street sweeper, who seems permanently bent in the back from his occupation, was walking in circles sweeping refuse into small piles with his pine needle broom. He has no pail and therefore no worrisome bother about collecting the refuse he sweeps up. He was told another worker with a sturdier back would come along soon to collect the neat piles of his endeavor. Yet, the street sweeper never did encounter the man with the pail and suspects the wind, not a fellow worker, simply blows his piles away each night. Não faz mal, he reasons. Not to worry. As long as there is dirt, there is work.

Smitty notices that the street sweeper smokes cigarette butts dropped by the Englishmen, sidesteps an occasional dog turd and urinates in the gutter. When he can, the street sweeper likes to watch the colorful fishing boats come and go in the distance. For his work, he receives a meal and a bed for the night at the bodega. No one knows where he gets his money for wine, because he doesn't beg and doesn't borrow.

What ultimately brought Smitty to this backward country was no longer as important as why he decided to extend his stay in the Algarve. Because he spent his days watching an old man grow older and regret more than dying the far grimmer prospect his life might end utterly worthless. Smitty was torn between writing the story he came to Portugal to pursue, and the story he now felt compelled to create. If Copper Jack still harbored doubts about his worthiness as a subject matter, Smitty was finally convinced Copper's life was a story worth telling.

It would not be the story Copper expected. It would be a love story. A love for life and for his country, but mostly a love for the woman of his dreams, something he felt deeply in his heart even as he struggled to articulate his feelings to Tookie's satisfaction. Smitty suspected Copper feared trying to win Tookie back with romance, more than he feared dying. A duel was the easy way out. He could face death, yet not the thought of courting Tookie all over again, only to lose her in the end. Smitty guessed Copper's sudden preoccupation with embellishing his 'legacy' was probably a need to satisfy Tookie's ego more than his own.

Dwelling on Copper's vulnerabilities helped steer Smitty away from his own private turmoil, so he pounded away at the typewriter hour after hour with a renewed sense of purpose. When he finally paused in prolonged silence to reread the text and decide if what he'd written was intelligible, Virgo entered his room unannounced.

"Are you trying to write her back into, or out of, your life?" she asked.

"Would it matter to you one way or the other?"

"Only if it mattered to you."

Smitty cherished this polite indifference in their relationship. Up to now, they both had chosen to remain intimate strangers. So far, Smitty could share as much or as little as he pleased without Virgo passing judgment or trying to change the way he was. Likewise, Virgo knew whatever she shared or didn't share was fine with him. For the first time ever, Smitty recognized what it was that drove him into one innocuous love affair after another; when it was over, it didn't hurt. The affair could inspire his writing, but never get in the way of it.

"Actually, I was writing about Copper Jack just now," Smitty confessed.

"Then I am jealous," she teased him.

"As jealous as Copper Jack is of Tookie?" Smitty asked.

"I think it's smashing that he's still true blue to his wife after all these years, especially living in this adulterous community. That says a lot." Smitty disagreed.

"On the contrary, because you walked into my life, it occurs to me I need to remind Copper about the delights of having an uncomplicated, open-ended affair with a gorgeous woman like you."

"Has it been as good for you as it has for me?"

"Better," he admitted.

Smitty took Virgo into his arms as if he owned her. It was the way she liked it. If she fought back at all, it was only to make the moment richer.

It was hot for a spring day, but they held each other close long after it was over. Resting his head against her supple body, so quiet outside he could hear the bees buzzing in the hemlock beneath his window, it occurred to Smitty that perhaps the Algarve was the real land of hope and glory.

"You know, Smitty, you have never asked me much about my life," Virgo said, sounding hurt. Smitty dropped his arms to his sides and rolled over on his back staring up at the ceiling. He had heard this same refrain from other women.

"Maybe I can only concentrate on one story at a time," he offered unconvincingly. Turns out Smitty had bragged to himself too soon. He fought off the uneasy feeling their relationship was burrowing deeper than he intended. Without invitation, Virgo rolled over on her back, stared up at the same blank ceiling, and proceeded to bare her soul completely in Smitty's presence. Suddenly Smitty longed to return to the typewriter.

Her story was simple. She had left England for Portugal in search of the man who had walked out on her one day unannounced. "I always knew Eric was a frigging layabout, with other women, mostly. But it still came as a surprise to me when it happened. I tracked him as far as the Algarve, but he vanished into thin air by the time I got here. He was here just long enough to win the hearts of a couple of Portuguese maidens, apparently. So it sounds like Eric has evolved into quite the international womanizer, wherever he is," she said, sounding like she no longer cared.

"I stayed on here convincing myself he might backtrack and return to the Algarve one day. When in fact, the real reason I stayed is I simply couldn't face all the naysayers back home in the UK. From the very beginning, I had ample warning about Eric from several quarters, which I simply chose to ignore," she said, without a trace of bitterness or regret.

"And your occupation, you've never talked about your business here in the Algarve," Smitty asked, trying to change the subject from failed romance.

"I'm not lesbian, if that's what you're worried about. Neither are the ladies I'm in touch with. I do it for the money, and they do it because they are simply lonely. There is a dark side to every woman a man can never touch," she said mysteriously. When she had finished unveiling her life to Smitty, he said what came naturally…

"Good material for a story."

Virgo was miffed. "Don't want to wind up between your book covers, Smitty. Your arms would do for now." Smitty held her close again, more reluctantly this time, wondering when it would all have to end between them. As if reading his mind, she gave him a playful pinch between the legs. "How about another go at it? Or can't you get it up?" she challenged him.

While Copper Jack dwelled on the past and Smitty pondered his future, Virgo was the master of the here and now.

9

Adrift at Sea

Bustle thought about stuffing a message calling for help down the throat of an empty gin bottle and tossing it far out to sea. However, the larger question was: how to phrase the message so it captured the extreme urgency of his situation?

Deserted by his sea legs from the outset, he spent the majority of the voyage spilling his guts over the side of his beloved yacht. His stomach failed him, so had his navigational equipment, and finally the engine blew. When he lost all radio contact as well, he recalled the story of the Japanese infantryman during World War II, who had been cut off from the outside world and was found defending his foxhole several years later after the war had long-since officially ended. Bustle felt every bit as isolated.

A month out to sea, they had not sighted another ship or body of land since disembarking from their beloved Algarve. The Portuguese crew became restless and fired the cannon out of sheer boredom. As promised, the cannon backfired and the yacht was slowly taking on water. "In short," Bustle decided to say in his handwritten plea for help, "situation quite dire, willing to stuff it all for a game of darts and a dry pair of socks. Do send help post-haste, signed, Bilkington."

Bustle's personal misadventure was to remain an accurate barometer of England's own debacle on the war front. To a man, Britain had grossly underestimated Argentina's willingness to fight and her ability to do so. Two days after scoring the first hit of the war by sinking the Belgrano, Argentina retaliated by sinking the Sheffield. The initial euphoria on both sides soon hardened into grim and desperate determination. The situation quickly morphed into a serious shooting war nobody wanted.

With Bilkington adrift somewhere at sea, Frill Pimpton was adrift on land. Without Bustle's companionship, afternoon siesta became the loneliest time of day for Frill. Villagers shuttered shop and villa windows and filled smoky cafes with animated conversation. Streets smelled of char-broiled sardines. Farms were deserted and left to the scarecrows. A lonely shepherd might enjoy a flask of wine and a round of cheese under a shady tree with a trunk that fitted his spine, yet that was the only sign of life. For Frill, siesta was the time of day when she stayed indoors and drank the heaviest. Occasionally, she had a visitor.

The Portuguese farmer next door to her villa had a fondness for brandy, too fond to suit his wife. Frill called her his 'Donkey Woman' because of her unfortunate facial similarity and legendary stubbornness. Whenever she found her husband, Francisco, hitting the bottle during siesta, usually hiding out in the barn, she would chase him around the farmland with a broomstick raised menacingly above her head.

"Poor sod," Frill always said to herself in sympathy, whenever she saw the melodrama unfold from the front porch of her villa. On these occasions, it was Francisco's habit not to return to the fields after siesta. Instead, he would seek out refuge in the villa of the lonely English widow next door.

His afternoons with the 'Madame' were always a case of borderline rape. If he was shy with the English lady, he was also more than willing. Frill exhausted him and left the poor farmer without the desire or energy to satisfy Donkey-Woman at night, so his wife became understandably suspicious. One afternoon, Donkey-Woman followed Francisco to Frill's villa. With broomstick raised above her head, she entered the villa without knocking.

Donkey-Woman found Frill kneeling at the foot of her dead husband's portrait above the fireplace, begging permission to commit yet another transgression. Donkey-Woman saw Francisco's hat hanging on the coat rack by the front door and slipped silently down the hallway toward the bedroom.

Soon Frill heard the shouting begin and quickly cowered in the corner as the raucous behavior gravitated from the bedroom down the hallway in her direction. What she finally witnessed was a familiar sight: Donkey-Woman stalking her startled husband with the broomstick held high above her head. This time, however, Francisco had been caught butt-naked. A momentary pit-stop at the front door to collect his hat cost him a swift swat of the broom across his bare bum. He let out a violent yelp as he vacated Frill's villa, with Donkey-Woman in hot pursuit and yelling obscenities in Portuguese all the way to the farmhouse. Once again during siesta, Frill was left to her own devices.

With the hard realities of war settling in, Tookie also felt abandoned. Her sitting room was no longer the social hub of the Algarve. Copper's repeated outspoken criticism of the war had driven most of their remaining friends away for good. "I feel like a leper," she complained to Copper. "They're calling us sympathetic bean-eaters behind out backs."

Copper reacted by drawing more inward. In his resignation against the war and his effort to conjure up for Smitty the meaning of life, he was slowly driving the final wedge between himself and Tookie. Hunkered down and totally preoccupied, Copper reduced his world to the radius of an invalid: roughly the twenty-seven steps it took him to travel from his armchair to the bathroom and back again. Any sleep he snatched was in his armchair, upright and fitful. He ate once a day when the maid came because Tookie refused to wait on him hand and foot. He grew a gray and wiry beard which relieved him of having to shave each day and face himself in the mirror.

Tookie filled her lonely days with solemn walks along the beach, feeling neglected and looking longingly out to sea. Clearly, old age had not served Tookie and Copper well. Their golden years had tarnished, robbing them of each other's affection when they needed it most, and drawing unwanted attention to the warts in their marriage. Neither of them seemed able or willing to turn back the clock and recapture a better time in their lives together.

Even in distress, Tookie never seriously considered having an affair with Bustle. She was fond of his knack for making her laugh and feel alive, but she could not admit to an overpowering physical attraction for him. In the midst of her dilemma with nowhere else to turn, Tookie finally decided to pay Virgo a visit.

Both Virgo and Bustle viewed Tookie as the crown jewel of the Algarve. She stood alone among the other women in successfully eluding their advances. It was simply not her cup of tea. Like her husband Copper Jack, her self-imposed celibacy was common gossip. When she arrived at Casa Bodega and tried to slip upstairs to Virgo's room unnoticed, Liz saw her from behind the bar, arched her eyebrows and announced under her breath: "Another ship about to sink at sea." The remark fell on deaf ears for everyone at the bar but Smitty, who glanced over his shoulder just in time to see Tookie disappear at the top of the stairs.

"I don't follow you, Liz."

"Better follow Tookie, then. Or talk to Virgo. It's no business of mine," she shrugged. "My customers like a bartender who can be discrete."

Smitty and Liz were engaged in a long conversation about life on the Algarve and, of course, you couldn't talk about the Algarve without referencing Copper Jack. "He's not coping well, is he?" Liz asked, knowing Copper's parlor politics had disenchanted most of the locals and driven more business her way.

As each news bulletin from the wireless reported another sunken ship or fallen fighter plane, the crowd at the bar greeted the news like the score of a World Cup soccer match: "Brits five, Argies two," someone shouted deliriously. Liz and Smitty knew Copper was scoring the war in terms of body bags.

"Stubborn old coot," Liz continued. "Copper is probably home stewing over the fact that no one from Downing Street consulted him before going to war. Imagine such grandiose expectations from a self-educated pig farmer," she said, shaking her head in disbelief. Realizing she was being too tough on Copper, especially in front of his biographer, Liz back-pedaled somewhat on her criticism. "Let's just say, Copper's always been respected by his own kind. He never had the proper last name to get very far in the UK, anyway, but he did serve as the official voice of the local farmers union in Kent and was well on his way to becoming their representative in the House of Commons. Of course, then he got hooked up with Tookie, and the rest is history," she reminded Smitty, rolling her eyes for effect.

Smitty stared warily upstairs where Tookie had disappeared, while Liz tried hard to keep him focused on Copper. "He lost the support of the farmers finally because adultery is still considered messy business in jolly old England. Besides, Tookie could no longer tolerate the whispers of their wives and the accusing looks she received in the marketplace. So she and Copper up and walked away from it all: got married: sold the farm: said goodbye to his possible political career. Just like that," she said, snapping her fingers, "and for what? A rotten piece of crumpet, stealing him away to the Algarve to waste her husband's final years in luxurious exile."

"Liz, as we both know, you're not exactly open-minded when it comes to Copper and Tookie," Smitty said, standing up suddenly from his bar stool, putting money on the counter. "How can she call him a failure when it's she who failed Copper Jack? She can be poison, I tell you, and she's on her way to killing him off, if you want my opinion."

Smitty was maxed out on opinions relating to Copper Jack and didn't need more input from anyone on the subject. Instead, he excused himself and headed for the stairway.

"I wouldn't advise it, Yank," Liz warned, "might find out more than you and your book can stomach."

Despite Liz's warning, Smitty climbed the stairway anyway, on a mission to prevent disaster from happening. Was he reacting out of concern for Copper, Tookie, Virgo or himself? It was all too complicated to know for sure, yet doing nothing was not an option, he decided. When he put his ear to Virgo's door, he could make out clearly the sound of her velvety voice... "... and you will take a bold, adventuresome step toward satisfying your innermost desires."

Those words were enough to move Smitty to action. He entered Virgo's room without knocking and discovered Virgo sitting innocently on the sofa reading Tookie's open palm. Both ladies were fully composed and fully clothed. It was Smitty who suddenly felt like a naked boob as he began to withdraw from Virgo's room in hopes no one noticed.

"Don't look so distraught, Smitty," Virgo laughed and called after him. "I'm sure we could interest Tookie in a little ménage à trois."

Tookie concluded the "bold, adventuresome step" Virgo had prophesied translated into a trip for her back to the UK. She would stay with friends and relatives, she told Copper, "just until this spat with Argentina is over because I don't feel safe here, quite frankly."

Finally, it was done. Copper had managed to drive away his wife, his biographer and anyone he once called a friend. He was left with his Portuguese maid, the wireless and the war, which dragged on unexpectedly toward a third anguishing month. Copper became increasingly edgy about the war. With his villa and his life now completely empty, word of every British ship or Argentine aircraft to go up in flames prompted a visceral outburst simply to break the silence of his world and reaffirm his own existence again.

"Quit pissing about at sea, get on shore and end it," he shouted impatiently at the wireless. With a possible diplomatic solution now out of the question, the Argies vowed to fight to their death and their stranglehold on the Falklands capital of Port Stanley required nothing short of an all-out land invasion to remove them. While the whole world waited for a major assault on the strategic port, word came over the wires of a bloody, more disturbing prelude.

Like all famous battles, the name "Goose Green" rolled off the end of the tongue metaphorically, splashed onto the pages of history books before the blood had dried, inspiring premature celebration in the streets back home in the UK. Overlooked in the initial giddiness was the eventual outcome: well over a hundred Argies killed or wounded and only seventeen Brits dead. Copper was beside himself after hearing the sobering news. The World War II hero turned pacifist trembled with anger as he stood up from his armchair, cocked his right leg into the air, and put his slipper through the loud speaker of his wireless.

10

Tie a Yellow Ribbon

By the time Argentina surrendered las Malvinas to Britain at Port Stanley several days later, Copper Jack had also managed to make peace with himself. Recapturing Stanley required a miniature landing not unlike the grander D-Day invasion in which Copper participated years ago, but historical comparisons were a complete waste of his time. Copper no longer cared about hanging onto the past or embellishing his own personal legacy. He was fighting for his marriage and nothing else really mattered anymore.

A telegram from Tookie announced she would return to the Algarve now that the war had ended. In her absence, Copper discovered the heart did, in fact, grow fonder. He decided Tookie was more important to him than anything, and he promised to tell her in exactly those words when she returned, hoping his open confession would make a difference. He also had a few other surprises for Tookie up his sleeve.

You can't turn back the clock, he decided, but you can certainly wind it up again so it's ticking in real time. Copper begged the local dentist to fix him up with a shiny set of false teeth to brighten up his toothless, 'dish rag' mouth, as she called it and, for the first time in weeks, he actually showered and shaved. He even dusted off his old dance step, practicing alone in his slippers which squeaked across the hardwood floor like mice. He tried to keep step with his dance partner, a broomstick, as the music played from an antique Victrola, the contraption next to his armchair that replaced his beloved wireless. In the end, he preferred music in the house instead of the news, but decided he had lost a few steps on the dance floor. So, Copper selected a slower dance tune to compensate.

Fresh paint adorned the walls of the sitting room, fresh flowers waited in the dining room and a bottle of champagne chilled for her arrival. He asked the maid to put a crease in his slacks and Copper tied a yellow ribbon around Tookie's armchair to welcome her home. On the eve of her return, "His Majesty" had thought of everything.

"The stage is all set," Copper told Smitty confidently the next morning. They drank coffee at an outdoor café in the shadow of Prince Henry the Navigator, a statue of Portugal's famous explorer. Copper told Smitty he was finally prepared to take the risk, rediscovering the uncharted waters of romance, as foreign as it seemed to him. "Love is like fruit on the window sill. It can go bad waiting to ripen," he said.

In exchange for the chance to once again pick Copper's fertile mind, Smitty forgave him the unfortunate metaphor which had nothing to do with romance. During the Falklands War and Copper's self-ordained withdrawal from the outside world, Smitty came to miss these regular encounters with him. Today, Copper's coffee was generously laced with brandy which unleashed his tongue for the first time in months. Smitty couldn't resist using Copper's own bad metaphor to chide his good friend.

"Like fruit in the window sill, a book can also go bad waiting to ripen." Copper pursed his lips sheepishly at the reference.

"OK, Smitty, got your message. I do owe you an apology. You have every right to be upset. Simply have not been myself lately, hounded with troubles of every sort. Don't know what possessed me to commission you in the first place. I'd rather we were good mates going forward and forget all this rubbish about a book."

"Only if you agree to help me with the book I came to Portugal to write in the first place: a love story." Copper's eyes suddenly twinkled. "Well, on that subject you have certainly come to the right doorstep. Love has caused me most of my troubles," he grinned, flashing his new set of false teeth proudly. Copper leaned back in his chair, sipping his coffee laced with brandy and reaching hard for a better metaphor to capture an image of true romance. "Come to think about it, love is like a Portuguese bullfight," he suggested excitedly. Smitty sat back in his chair uncomfortably, wincing and waiting for the other shoe to drop.

"Hear me out on this one, Smitty. In Portugal, as in Spain, bullfighting is sport. But in this country, it's also poetry. While a Spanish bullfighter plods around on foot, waving a colorful bedspread and a sharp lance at the bull to earn a few *olés* from the crowd, Portuguese bullfighters ride on horseback, which requires real skill and daring. Spaniards take fewer chances and always butcher the bull in the end. In Portugal, the bull lives to see another day. Always gets a second chance." Copper paused to let Smitty complete the thought.

"A second chance, as in romance?" Smitty asked.

"Always knew you were a smart lad."

"With such a great teacher, how could I be anything but?" Smitty laughed and Copper laughed along with him.

A breeze off the Atlantic wafted over the village square and Copper savored the notion that he, too, was giving Tookie a second chance. A question he could not answer was, *would she return the favor?*

"Nice metaphor, Copper Jack," Smitty said, giving him credit as well as a reminder. "Just remember, in a duel, only the survivor gets a second chance."

"May not need a duel, Smitty, if I can win Tookie back with my heart instead of a pistol."

"Are you sure she's worth the bother?"

"I'd do a lot of things differently second time around, but not my decision to marry Tookie. She's the best thing ever happened to me and I'll win her back anyway I can." Copper leaned across the table and whispered to Smitty for emphasis. "Never too late for you to do the same."

Smitty shook his head in disagreement. "Once you've lost that feeling, you can never get it back, no matter how many times you apologize, or how many duels you fight. You've simply got to turn the page."

"Easy for you to say, I'm an old man. The thought of walking out and starting over scares the bile out of me. At my age I can't imagine setting up shop with a new piece of crumpet. Took too long to train this one," he chuckled.

"Come on, Copper. All this agony over one woman is senseless. Every species on earth is polygamist by nature."

"Except swans, they always mate for life. Guess I'm one of those unfortunate creatures."

"O.K., for the sake of argument, just imagine for a moment having an affair with Frill Pimpton."

"She's probably a great roll in the hay, but I gave up farming long ago," Copper joked.

"And Liz? I know for a fact there's magic between the two of you."

"Reverend Pat's wife? Even as an atheist, I would never steal from the church this close to meeting my Maker – just in case there is one."

"O.K., how about Virgo, someone younger?"

"And cheat on my best friend? I do appreciate you trying to fix me up with someone, lad. Lord knows I could never do it on my own. But only one prescription makes sense for me and, fortunately, she's on the next plane to Portugal."

The sun rose in the sky heading toward siesta time, and Smitty and Copper graduated from coffee to cerveza. Copper continued to talk freely about his life and Smitty finally described the book he was writing. The love story Smitty described sounded very familiar, but Copper pretended not to notice.

Smitty accepted Copper's silence as his modest approval of Smitty's work in progress. When they finally stood up from their chairs, shook hands and left the square in opposite directions, Copper Jack was flashing his shitty little grin again and showing off his new false teeth. He would have his legacy after all.

Postwar activities lingered on at the bodega where Smitty returned soon after his meeting with Copper. Patriotic tunes played non-stop from the wireless behind the bar. Discussion among the Brits revolved around exaggerated war exploits, past and present. As a result of the never-ending celebration, Liz had trouble keeping the bar stocked with gin. "Had the war lasted any longer," she told Smitty when he walked into the bar, "my customers would get their first taste of your American prohibition."

In the weeks ahead, the world would sober up again. Margaret Thatcher, riding a new crest of popularity, would soon face a national rail strike and watch England's economy spiral downward thanks to the added war debts. In the aftermath of victory, customers at the bodega would soon resume their mournful passing of a once great empire.

When Smitty shared with Liz some of the details of his breakthrough meeting with Copper, she added a layer of context to what he had learned. "Kipling describes Copper better than anyone can. Ever read his poem, 'The Thousandth Man?" she asked. Smitty shook his head, prompting her recital:

"One man in a thousand, Solomon says,
    Will stick more close than a brother.
    And it's worthwhile seeking him half your days
    If you find him before the other.
    Nine hundred and ninety-nine depend
    On what the world sees in you,
    But the Thousandth man will stand your friend
    With the whole round world agin you."

"The Thousandth man, Smitty, that's Copper Jack. "It's not always what a man accomplishes, but the values he represents. I just don't think Tookie appreciates who this man really is."

Smitty did not admit to feeling sympathetic. He was not out to eulogize Copper or gloss over his shortcomings for which there were many. As he did with Virgo, Smitty preferred to keep his relationships at all times at arm's length to maintain his objectivity. The problem was, the more Smitty got to know him, Copper Jack kept welling up larger than life.

"So when is Tookie due back in town?" Liz asked.

"Tonight, as a matter of fact."

Liz sighed. "Somehow, I hoped she wouldn't come back at all. Not that there ever was a chance for me, mind you. Just don't like to see a man of that caliber eat away at himself over a woman who will never be good enough for him."

"Even if I agreed with you Liz, the important thing is Copper doesn't see it that way."

"He doesn't see at all anymore. That's the point. He needs someone to take care of him."

Copper panicked when he heard a knock at the door. It was too early for Tookie to arrive and he was still touching up around the house. When he opened the door and saw Frill Pimpton, he was relieved, but only momentarily. "I'm here because Tookie and I have a lady's agreement," Frill explained. "She asked me to watch out for you while she was away. Finally got up my courage."

"How touching," Copper said doubtfully. By now Frill was close enough to Copper to breathe heavily on him with stale and saturated breath, slurring her words along the way.

"See here, Frill. Your house-call is a bit tardy. War's over and Tookie's due home any minute now to take care of me. So your services are no longer needed. I will have to send you packing. Can't afford giving my wife the wrong impression upon her return." Copper put a coaxing hand on her shoulder, but Frill whirled around suddenly and let her blouse fall open, exposing her braless breasts. Copper did all he could do under the circumstances. She was in no condition to drive and he didn't have time to drive her home himself. So he poured Frill another drink or two until she passed out, so he could carry her peacefully off to bed in the guest room to let her sleep it off. He would figure out later how to explain Frill's presence to Tookie.

Smitty left Liz at the bar talking to herself, climbed the stairs to Virgo's room and felt the need to continue the conversation about Copper.

"Virgo, it's not like I didn't try. I even suggested having an affair would be healthy for him," Smitty divulged, "but you know Copper, true blue all the way. I even mentioned you might be available." Smitty knew it was the wrong thing to say the moment the words left his mouth.

"How dare you, Smitty! You are not my pimp! And I'm not some character in your book!"

"It would have been a good cause. You do as much for the women around here. Besides, I thought you were liberated. You're suddenly acting very domestic."

"I haven't seen you for a while, have I? A lot of thoughts have been running through my head that I haven't had the chance to share with you."

"Don't worry. Other than Copper today, no one else has seen me either. I've been working around the clock."

"When the typewriter stops, you never used to lock your door," Virgo complained. Casa Bodega and the Algarve had finally become too small for Smitty. The writer's curse is he needs to get close enough almost to smell the subject he's writing about, yet not so close it suffocates him. Smitty was finding it hard to catch a breath these days, especially when Virgo was in a mood to lecture him.

"I know why it never works out for you, Smitty. You are willing to get involved up to a point, but it must always be on your terms, preferably at arm's length. I'm convinced you would be ecstatic to get in my pants whenever you wanted as long as you didn't have to touch me. You want have total control as you do with the puppets in your book. Fact is, as a writer, you don't have a clue how to handle real flesh and blood. If you don't have feelings of your own, what gives you the right to tamper with the feelings of others?"

It had been a long time since anyone had bothered to hold a mirror up to Smitty. When situations like this become unbearable, his next move was usually out the door and into someone else's bed. Men and women were good for one another, he believed, as long as they didn't share too much of themselves. For a writer, he harbored a natural distrust for words and feelings. Simple seduction, on the other hand, was silent. So, in the end, Smitty had to admit to preferring body language over language itself.

On this occasion, however, it was Virgo who took the offensive. She wrestled Smitty to bed and tore off his clothes, trying to get under the skin of a man who kept pushing her away. Soon she was on top of him and bearing down on his body angrily, with eyes that glared wildly at him even as they filled with tears. When Smitty finally responded and took control of her body, Virgo's eyes glazed over and rolled back into her head, her eyelids twitching as a magical feeling shot throughout her body like electricity. "Sometimes you make me want to jump out of my skin even while I'm trying to get under yours," she said breathlessly, rolling over to his side and falling fast asleep.

Smitty relished the sudden quiet of her breathing. Just when he thought he dodged a bullet, she woke up again and unburdened her conscience once again. "Eric's back," she stated calmly, without a show of emotion. "Saw him at the bar. Didn't approach him so I have no idea where his head's at these days. Does it matter to you one way or another?"

Just like that, the trap was set. Smitty knew if he said yes, it matters, Virgo would be his, forever. He knew because he had crossed that bridge many years ago. Actually, he never made it across the bridge because he could not mouth the words that would make all the difference in the world.

Smitty dressed slowly as Virgo remained silent, giving him every opportunity to answer her question. His only answer was to shut the bedroom door behind him on his way to nowhere.

Copper Jack hummed to himself contentedly when he heard a second knock at his front door. Tookie had forgotten her key, he decided, but she arrived right on time. He surveyed the dining room and parlor proudly one last time before approaching the front door with extra bounce in his step. He flashed a final toothy grin in the mirror before opening the door.

Bilkington Bustle was the last person on earth Copper expected, or wanted, to see. No one had seen or heard from Bustle since he departed on his strange odyssey three months ago, and Copper couldn't have been happier. The voyage went way off course, Bustle explained, and delivered him only as far as the Azores, where his yacht put up for badly needed repairs. Bustle had just returned home having missed the war entirely. But he missed Tookie even more.

"Marvelous! Marvelous!" Bustle exclaimed, using his signature greeting, much to Copper's chagrin. "As you can imagine, desperately need a gin and tonic, old sport, to clear the salt water from my pipes. By the way, is Tookie about?" he asked, moving uninvited into the sitting room.

"She's out of the country at the moment. I'll get you a drink, but you really do have to be going soon," Copper lied, hoping to dismiss Bustle as soon as possible. Copper's hands were shaking with fury when he returned with the drink. Not surprisingly, Bustle's banter about the war would leave one to believe he directed it.

"The last war was difficult, no question. But this war was nearly the death of me," he exaggerated. "Mutinous crew, foul weather, a cannon ball in the side." As Copper expected, Bustle was ready to take his rightful place in the history books.

Somehow, Copper knew he needed to keep Bustle from ruining Tookie's homecoming. If he possessed any arsenic, he would have poisoned Bustle's drink without flinching. Suddenly, Copper came up with a brilliant idea. Perhaps he could persuade the lonely seaman to take Frill off his hands and, preferably, off the premises before Tookie arrived. However, before Copper's ingenious idea could turn misfortune in his favor, he heard another familiar voice enter the sitting room.

"Bilkington!" Tookie shouted. "You've returned safely!"

"And so have you, my dearest."

Copper felt weak in the knees with de ja vu. Tookie and Bustle were embracing again in his sitting room, just as they had before the war broke out. Not even the war had changed anything. With Tookie's back to Copper, all he could see was Bustle's sneering face resting against her shoulder, and Bustle's hands perched proudly on each handle of her hips, which looked decidedly thinner than Copper could last remember.

The day ended as it began, with Smitty and Copper sharing a few drinks, this time at the bodega.

They stumbled upon one another by accident this time, two jilted lovers drinking whisky straight up, which burned away like a branding iron any feelings they had, good or bad. Only after numbing the pain deep inside their intestines could they bring themselves to talk about it.

"You called it right, mate," Copper said in a hushed tone. "Why agonize with all the free crumpet running loose?"

"You hit the nail on the head, Copper," Smitty countered. "I had in my hands the one mermaid in the sea that mattered, and I let her slip away," he lamented for the first time to anyone. Liz saw the warning signs, kept the whisky coming, and finally dared to ask the only question she cared about:

"Did Tookie make it home?" Without hesitation, Copper removed his new set of false teeth and threw them against the back wall of the bar. His teeth shattered into a million pieces, tinkling against one another like loose piano keys as they fell to the floor. "You look more like yourself already," Liz noted.

11

Something Old, Something New

Now it was Copper's turn to prowl the beach alone in search of answers. He crouched occasionally to run his fingers across chunks of driftwood washed ashore and worn smooth, like the leftover fragments of life …the bare bones of who you were: a war veteran, an ambulance driver, a pig farmer and like skeletons picked clean of what you were not: a lord, a Member of Parliament, a Prime Minister.

Copper put aside his fear of the ocean, rolled up his pant legs to his knees and waded bravely into the shallow water. Waves tugged at his naked ankles and washed out to sea his momentary footprints in the sand. Off the coast of Portugal, his final legacy bobbed and weaved elusively, gasping for air. Copper was without a life buoy.

When all is said and done, you are who you are in the eyes of the one person you love the most. No one else counts as much. And whatever they say behind your back doesn't really matter. So when Tookie packed her bags and moved in with Bustle, Copper hurt too deeply to ask the question, why? Go forward, he told himself, turn the page. Instead, he found himself squeezing the scraps of driftwood tightly, like vivid memories of their life together.

How carefree it had been for Copper and Tookie when they left England behind, Copper recalled. They weren't spring chickens anymore even as they looked forward to a better life together but for a pair of disillusioned divorcees, they felt as idealistic and as love struck as do first-time heart throbs. With shiny new wedding rings on their fingers and all their worldly belongings tossed willy-nilly into the back of a caravan, they were suddenly as liberated as the gypsies cluttering the back roads of the English countryside.

Their new life was a complete and refreshing break with the past: the war they survived, the failed marriages they endured, the crimes of adultery they dared to commit in the name of love. They had made one final pass through their old neighborhood, the suffocating community of Kent, and smelled fresh air for the first time in their lives as their car and caravan pulled out of town for the last time.

The best way to shed old layers of skin, they decided, was to head south for warmer weather. They arrived first in the south of France, a place on earth that smiled approvingly on romance of any kind, with no questions asked. The countryside and people of Provence opened up their hearts to Copper and Tookie as their caravan rocked and rolled deliriously from campsite to campsite. They enjoyed the company of drifters like themselves because every day brought unexpected people from all walks of life. Each sunset found them sitting by the communal campfire, and in the arms of the one they loved.

"Like your cowboys, Yank, with their home on the range," is how Copper described his honeymoon to Smitty.

"Better than our cowboys," Smitty was quick to correct him. "Cowboys only had their horses to keep them company."

After exhausting half of his days fighting for his country, his farm and his woman, Copper finally possessed everything he wanted out of life. Tookie, it turns out, was still looking. You can take the lady out of England, not England out of the lady. A stately, spirited thoroughbred like Tookie inherited a natural craving for a life of royalty: the expansive wardrobe, the villa crawling with servants, endless tea-parties served on real china. The good life held little attraction for Copper. His fingernails were still dirty with fertile Kent soil, yet he bowed to the wishes of the woman he loved.

With an eye on settling down to a life of elegance in some distant far-off place, Copper and Tookie pushed as far south on the continent as their caravan would carry them, often on two wheels around the perilous mountain roads of the Spanish Pyrenees, before landing in their safe haven on the southern tip of Portugal. Their new life began where the old life left off: under the flag of England, which fluttered into view atop a thriving colony of Brits on Millionaire Hill. For Copper Jack, the honeymoon soon would be over.

From the sale of Copper's farmland in Kent they could afford to live comfortably off the interest and retire to a modest villa at the foot of Millionaire Hill. Their nearest neighbors were Portuguese, not English, so it wasn't the most desirable address in town. So the road from Millionaire Hill to the village passed by their doorstep, therefore, the proper visitors always called at the Jacks' house on their travels up or down the hill.

Of the two view windows from the Jack's villa, one pointed to the village allowing Copper Jack to study the curious ways of the Portuguese with growing admiration. The other window faced Millionaire Hill and fanned

Tookie's growing jealousy of the English who could afford to live there. Now, for better or for worse, she was about to become one of them.

A wave rose up suddenly and knocked Copper off his feet. In an instant, the strong currents pulled him under. Reality sank in as his head dropped below water. His nostrils burned and Copper knew he was sinking once again. However, the survival instincts that carried him safely through the war and pulled him out of the English Channel on many occasions, came to his rescue once again. He dog-paddled feverishly until he felt his bare feet touch sand, then scrambled back to shore, chilled and angry, yet also invigorated with a new sense of resolve.

Understandably, Bilkington Bustle had lost interest completely in the duel even though the whole idea was his own. Tookie had fallen into his lap without a fight. So Copper was left to get even with Bustle the only way he could. However, the object of Copper's revenge, Frill Pimpton, was taking Bustle's affair with Tookie as hard as Copper. He arrived at Frill's villa to find her passed out on the floor. The empty gin bottle at her side was her constant companion. The woman Copper had come to seduce looked as pathetic as he did.

"Go ahead, Copper," Frill said, waking up long enough to recognize the anger in his eyes. "If it will make you feel any better, I'll just lay here and take it. I know it will make me feel better." Frill spread her legs as if to make good on the offer, and passed out again. Copper lifted her gently into bed.

Still cold and wet from the ocean, Copper was tired of spending nights alone without Tookie. He left Frill's bedroom, returned to her living room, and built himself a roaring fire. He found a spare blanket, a fresh bottle of gin and stretched out on Frill's sofa. Gradually, the warmth from the gin and the hearth made Copper drowsy. He dozed off thinking only of Tookie. He remembered the touch of her skin. Sure the skin stretched and appeared more wrinkled with age, yet the touching and petting late in life means so much more than the huffing and puffing of youth, Copper realized. You touch each other's skin at this juncture, not to smooth the wrinkles away, but for good luck, to help you ward off the vagaries of life that descend upon you without your consent.

At first he thought the naked body pressing him against the sofa was the Tookie of his dreams but Copper immediately realized the heavy breath in his face could only be Frill Pimpton's. "Be honest. Have you ever slept with any woman other than Tookie?" Frill whispered in his ear.

"Not since we've been married."

"You have now," Frill smiled victoriously.

Sleep was one thing, Copper decided, sex was an entirely different matter. One could forgive Frill for not knowing the difference in her current condition. So, once she dozed off again, Copper crawled out from under her on the couch, grateful nothing happened, and stretched out his blanket in front of the fireplace until the next morning. From the dwindling light of the hearth, Copper noticed above the fireplace the portrait of Frill's former husband, Freddy, hanging backwards for this special occasion just in case she got lucky. At least someone was spared the pain of the moment.

Tookie walked out on the balcony of Mrs Bustle's bedroom, looking off in the distance for some sign of life in her old villa at the bottom of the hill. Since their separation, she had trouble sleeping. A glimpse of light from Copper's reading lamp would give her solace and help her return to bed and find sleep. Unfortunately, the villa at the foot of the hill stood in total darkness.

When she returned to her bedroom and finally fell asleep, like Copper, Tookie was hounded by fond remembrances, such as a cool August night just like tonight, many years ago in England, when she had frolicked delightfully in the back of Copper's ambulance. They couldn't afford a hotel room or risk being seen together since they were both married, so they parked the ambulance on a dead end road at the end of the village. To reserve the ambulance for the evening, Copper subjected himself to on-call duty and hoped a radio emergency would not suddenly interrupt his amorous intentions.

The night was overcast without a star in sight, but Copper managed to take care of everything else. The smell of champagne and flowers in the back of the ambulance overcame the smell of formaldehyde. He pulled the curtains on the ambulance windows and lit a candle. The flame flickered throughout the evening as Tookie melted into the arms of her ambulance driver. They attacked one another with voracious sexual appetites, certain they possessed no more than a few precious moments before a case of appendicitis relayed over the intercom would interrupt them. However, the fates cooperated on that magical evening, blessing the world with exceedingly good health. No emergency call interrupted their passion.

Gradually, the back of the ambulance began to shudder and shake from side to side as two lovers gained momentum, just as two surprised drunks staggered out onto the street from some nearby pub.

"I say. Isn't that Copper Jack's hospital wagon?" one drunk asked the other.

"Why would he park on a dead-end street, unless he's waiting for us?" the second drunk said, smiling at his own joke.

"Must be a bloody 'mergency of some kind. Look at her shimmy. And the windows all fogged up," observed the first drunk.

"Didn't hear no fuggin' siren," the second drunk noticed.

A sudden knock at the rear window brought activity inside the ambulance to a screeching halt. Belatedly, Copper emerged from the back of the ambulance and quickly slammed the tailgate shut.

Tookie remembered laughing under her breath as she overheard the conversation outside.

"Epileptic fit," Copper assured the two drunks and pointed toward the ambulance. "Touch and go. Must rush her home to bed, to the ward, I mean," he said, clearing his throat and blushing in darkness. "Cheerio, mates."

Finally, to mark the romantic occasion, sirens blared in Tookie's honor as they drove through the streets of Kent and red lights flashed from the top of her chauffeur-driven ambulance.

"Home, James," she said to her limousine driver.

The hand squeezing Tookie's shoulder woke her up. Bustle's touch was still strange to her. You don't sign up for an adulterous courtship following years of relatively blissful marriage, only to throw it all away on a whim. Tookie's motives were clear. She married young once. She married Copper for love. Now, she was running out of time if she was finally going to marry for money.

She knew Bustle collected a tidy sum from his wife's insurance policy on top of the generous pension he received as a retired civil servant of the Queen. Finally, she was well aware Bustle's lawyers were pressing Bustle's claim back in the UK that, rather than his brother's whore of a wife, he should be the lawful heir to his recently deceased brother's estate. In short, Bustle could soon provide for Tookie a rich lifestyle Copper simply couldn't match.

She liked the fact that Bustle's maid and gardener came every day instead of occasionally... not to mention the impeccable villa grounds and being waited on hand and foot. Bustle also bought her an entirely new wardrobe, suggesting Tookie's life was ahead of her, not ancient history. In the end, she needed more than the treasure trove of fond memories with Copper Jack to jumpstart each and every day.

For now, Bustle was deliberately patient with her. Tookie shunned his bed at night, opting for the privacy of her own bedroom. During the day, Bustle spent much of his time golfing at the Club, so Tookie had complete run of the villa and the servants. Bustle even gave Tookie carte blanche completely to redecorate the villa. "The place could use some cheering up with the missus passing on," he insisted. So Tookie threw herself whole-heartedly into her new life, with one exception. When it came to consummating their romance in the bedroom, Tookie was in no hurry. Past experience told her she needed time to give her feelings a true test, and plenty of leeway to understand what really mattered in love and life.

12

Casa Bodega

Copper Jack finally agreed to take a room at Casa Bodega at Liz's insistence. News of his separation from Tookie spread quickly through the community. As soon as Reverend Pat left town on business, Liz charged into Copper's sitting room unannounced and physically pulled him from his armchair, "Before you become part of the fabric," she demanded.

At the bodega, Liz would make sure Copper got three square meals every day, monitor his drinking and smoking, and hide Copper from Frill Pimpton at all cost. When he finally recovered from missing Tookie, Liz would be waiting in the wings for him. At least that was her plan.

Copper found life at the bodega a cross between country club elegance and nursing home callousness. He tossed and turned on a lumpy mattress and suffered the meals which were always served under a cloud of lumpy gravy. On the other hand, the linens were fresh every day and the meals, if tasteless, were at least hot and served regularly. All Copper really wanted and needed was to be left alone, of course, Liz would have none of that. First, the doctor called.

"I honestly thought only whores made house-calls anymore," Copper said, greeting the doctor sarcastically.

"If that's your wish, Copper, I'm sure Casa Bodega can accommodate you," the doctor said, pulling a stethoscope out of his black bag, "but first let's first make sure your heart is up to it."

"It's broken," Copper admitted, removing his shirt begrudgingly.

"On the contrary, strong as a bull, maybe too strong," the doctor reported, listening closely to the rapid thump of Copper's heartbeat. "How's the blood pressure these days?"

"Boiling," Copper said.

"Take a deep breath," the doctor ordered, ignoring Copper's attitude. He moved the stethoscope from Copper's chest to his lower back, asking Copper to inhale, exhale and cough each time he moved the instrument. "You still smoke like a chimney, don't you? Any discomfort anywhere?"

"Only the bloody knife sticking out my back."

"And how are the bowels?"

"With the food they serve here? You've got to be joking."

The doctor removed a small flashlight from his bag and shined it into Copper's pupils. "How are the eyes lately?"

"Color red most of the time."

Finally, the doctor put away the tools of his trade and closed his black bag. "Ok, here's the deal," the doctor prescribed. "You need more exercise and less of everything else. No smoking, drinking or women," he said, smiling at his last comment.

"Sounds like a clean bill of health to me," Copper said stubbornly, trying to turn the tables on anyone daring to give him advice at this point in his life.

Following the doctor's visit, Virgo was the next person Liz ordered to visit his room at the bodega. "The time has passed for your massage," Virgo announced.

"Over my dead body and yours, thank you very much."

"I have specific orders, Copper."

"And I have my scruples."

"Keep your pants on then. I'll work around them."

Virgo led Copper, pissing and moaning, from the chair to the bed. However, once Virgo's fingers began to penetrate the stiff muscles in his back, Copper's disposition improved considerably.

"Give into it, Copper," Virgo urged.

"Not used to letting my guard down. Bad habit from the war," he acknowledged.

"Feels better already, doesn't it?" Virgo insisted, as she could feel Copper begin to relax.

"Maybe I will take my pants off after all," Copper teased.

Virgo's nimble hands danced magically up and down his spinal cord and, finally, to the nape of his neck. Copper's skin sprouted goose bumps and shivered with delight. Within minutes, Copper's whole body became putty in her hands. "No matter what they say about you, Virgo, you certainly know your business," Copper sighed.

"Do you mind if I know your business? What if I read your palm?"

"I don't put much stock in superstition. A man makes his own luck."

"Until a moment ago, you didn't put much stock in massage."

Virgo ran her fingers gently across his palm and Copper relented. She studied his life line at great length. After a long silence, Copper's curiosity got the best of him.

"All right, lass. Humor an old man. What's it say, then?"

Virgo shook her head and pulled back from him. "Like you said, I wouldn't put much stock in it," she agreed, but the worry on her brow was troubling to him. She continued to massage Copper's body until he surrendered to a deep sleep. Virgo left the room wishing she had never come.

Smitty drank alone at the bar when Virgo sat down next to him. They both stared ahead like total strangers. "Drinking early in the day like the English, I see" Virgo said.

"Celebrating my return to the States shortly," he said, dropping a bomb on her. After a long silence, Virgo turned to face him directly, almost demanding a retraction.

"Running back to the States with your tail between your legs makes absolutely no sense whatsoever," she said disgustedly. "Especially since Eric and I are not getting back together," she said, making sure Smitty understood the profoundness of his decision. Smitty found her eyes deeper, more magnetic than he remembered.

"Winter's around the corner. I'll have been in the Algarve for almost a year and my work here is pretty much finished. Unlike the novelist Tom Wolfe, I'm going to prove you can go home again."

Virgo would have none of it. "You're drunk, Smitty. Cut with the literary crap. What's it mean in clear Queen's English?" she asked, searching his face for answers.

"It means goodbye, Virgo," he said, taking a final gulp of his drink before standing up to leave.

"You're so full of yourself. Running away again, are you? Not even a dying friend can change your mind," she said, playing her trump card in the end. Smitty paused before leaving the bar, prepared to hear her out. "I've just come from Copper's room. The sign is in his palm," she announced.

"Come clean, Virgo," Smitty said impatiently. "I say mumbo jumbo. You're swallowing the tripe from your own sales pitch."

"Surely you know about the duel."

"I'm the one that told you, remember? Besides, that's all water under the bridge now. And good riddance, I say. Copper would have gotten himself killed over her."

"According to his palm, the duel's back on," she warned.

"Sorry, Virgo, but your fortune cookie has grown a little stale."

"Oh, really, look at Tookie, following her heart's desire, just as I predicted. And don't forget what I read in the palm of your hand," she reminded him.

"Read into my palm, you mean. Still haven't figured out if it's you or Copper who's supposed to change my life."

"Either way, the prediction's accurate."

Without taking his eyes off Virgo, Smitty ordered a bottle of champagne. "The best you've got, Liz. And two glasses." Smitty poured them both a glass of champagne and Virgo wondered why.

"If you're leaving the country, why are we celebrating?" she asked, puzzled.

Smitty offered a toast. "To a friend and a most surprising friendship."

"Is she why you are going back? The Dark Woman in your life?" When Smitty refused to answer the question, Virgo answered for him. "You never fooled me, Yank. I fooled myself. Thought I could step in and somehow take her place."

"All I know about relationships, Virgo," Smitty finally responded, "is that when Tookie is in Copper's arms, devil be damned. Copper is everything he ever wanted to be and with very few regrets. Without Tookie, he's nobody and he knows it. Personally, I'm jealous of Copper. I've never been able to admit that I needed someone else."

"I thought so. Sounds like you're going back to the States to try again."

"And to keep trying, this time," Smitty confessed.

"Well damn you, then," she announced defiantly. "I'll keep trying, too. If I have to fight for you, I will."

To avoid the crush of the bodega crowd during siesta, Smitty and Virgo took their battle and bottle of champagne with them as they mounted the stairway together.

Copper awoke from his nap in a funk and saw Liz standing at his bedside hovering over him. "Did you sleep well?" she asked. His nostrils picked up the deadly smell of gravy steaming up from a nearby lunch tray Liz had delivered personally.

"I have a complaint for management."

"Good. You sound like you're old cantankerous self again."

"Stop making like I'm sick," he demanded, sitting up in bed.

"Doc said you were mean as ever."

"I suppose Virgo's visit was also you're idea."

"You weren't flattering yourself otherwise, I hope," she needled him. Copper got out bed and stomped across the room to the window and looked out.

"This is a winery, Lizard. Fine wine needs time to breathe. So let me breathe, woman!" Copper tried to throw open the French doors to get some air, but the doors were locked. Copper turned around and faced Liz. "Do you honestly think I'd jump from the balcony?" he asked.

"Just think we are all a little bit jumpy after what happened to Mrs Bustle," Liz explained. Copper lit a cigarette, recalled the doctor's warning, and snuffed it out just as quickly.

"Honestly, do I look like a man who's ready to pack it in?"

"You just look like a man to me," Liz said, smiling lasciviously.

"Look, Liz. I know what you are on to," Copper said. "You want my body, or what's left of it. But it won't work. It's too soon. And we are both married."

"That's what I came to talk about, Copper. Please sit down and listen." Liz led Copper by the hand to the edge of the bed as Copper lit his cigarette again. He knew he needed a smoke no matter what the doctor said. "Tookie called me at the bodega," Liz began. "She wanted to make a reservation for a wedding."

"Perhaps to restate our wedding vows?" Copper tried to pretend.

"Not quite, Copper."

After a long draw from his cigarette and a longer pause from Liz, Copper asked the inevitable. "So what's the date of the wedding?" he asked, in a voice barely audible.

"No date, just inquiring about the Reverend's availability to do the marriage ceremony."

Copper paced the floor of the room, expressionless. Liz sat on the edge of the bed waiting for Copper to explode, to cry out, take her in his arms, but Copper did nothing. Events were moving too quickly for him. He stopped long enough to ground his cigarette butt with his shoe against the floor and glanced absently out the window just as Bustle's car approached the bodega. Even with a second look, Copper couldn't quite make out the woman sitting next to Bustle in the car. He didn't really need to. To make peace with Liz, Copper lifted the lid of the neglected lunch tray and took a deep, obligatory whiff.

"Beautiful," he lied, "but I'd rather have a drink. Let's go downstairs."

Smitty and Virgo drained the bottle of champagne and slowly savored the aftermath of their reunion. It was siesta, the time of day when British locals crowded the Casa Bodega bar seeking respite from the sun and satisfaction of their undying thirst for gin. Smitty and Virgo ignored the hubbub of activity and shrill laughter from the bar below, intent on listening to each other's breathing as the bedroom walls around them reflected the blinding sunlight of high noon. They had never made love in broad daylight before. They might never again.

"How can you up and leave what we have here?" Virgo asked Smitty, shifting her naked flanks his way.

Smitty ran his hand back and forth across her delectable peaks and valleys. He looked around the room with a sense of nostalgia. The familiar, welcome breeze always kicked up this time of day to help cool the room enough to allow him to write long into the hot Algarve afternoons. Some days he would join the crowd at the bar just to stay in touch with his subject matter, yet would always return to the typewriter later in the afternoon feeling heady and inspired.

Today, the intoxicating smell of the bodega, an aroma of overripe grapes and aged oak barrels from years gone by, colored his mood with both love and sorrow. The country of Portugal had been so kind to Smitty and the pages of text stacked neatly next to his typewriter were proof of his creative harvest. He was ready to share his writing with Copper Jack.

"At least I can walk away with fond memories and a sense of closure," Smitty finally responded.

"Damn your memories! What about my closure?" Virgo shouted, bolting upright from the bed and slinging a feather pillow across the room in frustration. Virgo lowered her eyes dejectedly as tears began to drop to her lap like fall leaves surrendering to the change of seasons. She was not unyieldingly beautiful, but Smitty still found her tempestuously attractive. Between sniffles, her naked breasts surged and sagged with each sigh of emotion, as she sat girlishly cross-legged in the middle of the bed. Smitty put his hand in her lap, catching some of the tears as they dropped, tenderly caressing her feet and calves, enjoying again the fullness of her thighs beneath his touch.

Virgo spoke in halting gasps of air that escaped from her lungs like the desertion she felt in her heart. "From the beginning, I got this childish, desperate notion in my head that you could write your books here, without distraction, free of the past and I would be at your side to support you. What more can you possibly want?" Smitty's strained silence granted her permission to continue. "Or, is the cruel truth, we all want what we can't have? You still want the Dark Woman. I want you. Copper wants Tookie. We all lose out in the end," she said, her voice trailing off into a whisper.

At the moment, Copper didn't want Tookie or a drink. He simply wanted revenge. The hated couple was easy to pick out of the crowd below. Halfway downstairs Copper caught a glimpse of the woman clinging affectionately to Bustle's arm. They stood behind friends seated at the bar of the bodega and chatted away amiably waiting for their drinks to be served. Someone offered her a seat, but she declined in order to move closer to Bustle and squeeze his arm more securely than before.

Their backs were completely turned to him as Copper approached them from behind. In a blind rage, Copper recognized only what he wanted to notice: the smart new dress and hat she wore, and the smell of strong perfume as he got closer. Copper could no longer control the pit in his stomach and shouted from the top of his lungs. "Bustle!" he screamed, as all conversation at the bar became frozen in time. When he screamed Bustle's name for a second time, all eyes in the bodega focused on the threat of Copper Jack.

In the split second that followed, Bustle and his lady friend spun around to address Copper, who searched her eyes in vain for any sign of sympathy or remorse. The surprise for Copper was that Frill Pimpton, not Tookie Jack, stood at Bustle's side. For Copper, Frill's presence was even more unsettling. To be made into a cuckold was one thing. Yet to have your unfaithful wife, Tookie, two-timed by Bustle and Frill in full public view before your very own eyes, and with a wedding to his former wife in the offing, Copper was beside himself with anger. He lunged suddenly at Bustle's throat and began choking him until the stunned crowd at the bar reacted and pulled Copper safely away from Bustle. As Bustle readjusted his necktie nervously, Copper issued a challenge to Bustle's honor publicly, so Bustle couldn't possibly back out now.

"So what's it going to be, Bustle?" he raged. "A gentleman's duel face-to-face, or a bullet in your backside without so much as a warning?"

"I have the best of both worlds, old chap," Bustle said, nodding at Frill. "Why should I ever put my life on the line?"

As Bustle scanned the disapproving faces of his fellow Brits at the bar, it was obvious public sentiment was on Copper Jack's side. Bustle's manhood, if not his life, was clearly on the line whether he wanted it that way or not. "Very well, then, as you wish," Bustle agreed, with a touch of resignation in his voice.

Having extracted from Bustle the public promise of revenge, Copper charged off in the direction of Millionaire Hill in search of Tookie.

13

Reunion of the Soul

Copper found her in Bustle's villa dressed in a long-flowing gown and bracing herself against the balustrade of a massive marble staircase, the classic pose of all the great actresses in all the great films of their generation. Tookie appeared to thoroughly enjoy her newly exalted position in society. "A stairway like this must play hell with your varicose veins," Copper called up from the ground level.

"I didn't hear you arrive," Tookie apologized.

"Then we're even," Copper said, keeping score. "I never heard you leave," he reminded her.

"Copper, what's done is done and there's no going back. Hope you haven't come to try to change my mind."

"Make up your own mind, woman. The man you are about to marry is holding court at the Casa Bodega bar arm-in-arm with Frill Pimpton." Tookie merely shrugged off the news.

"We can't very well expect him to change his ways overnight because we know boys will be boys."

Copper was astounded by Tookie's nonchalance. "You don't care, do you? Then let the scoundrel make a public mockery of us both, and a fool of you in particular." Tookie remained unperturbed.

"We'll see who the fool is at the end of the day, and that's why I'll never agree to share his bed."

"You expect me to believe you will marry a man you will never sleep with?"

"Not that it's your business anymore, Copper Jack. If it will comfort you in some odd way, no, I never plan to sleep with Bilkington."

"So what are your intentions behind this charade?" he asked.

"To have everything I ever wanted out of life."

"I thought so. You're after his bank account. Now it all makes sense." Copper sat down dejectedly on the bottom step of the marble staircase, surveying the plush surroundings in every direction.

Tookie navigated the stairway with great stature before sitting innocently next to him. For all the upheaval in their lives, at least her *Estée Lauder* perfume was familiar, he noticed. "What will you do with yourself now?" she asked Copper, sounding concerned.

"What did I ever do with myself? Probably get a new wireless since I bashed in the old one. I've been mucking around in the dark without one."

"So, it's still about you and your bloody world affairs when nobody else really cares. It's not me you're missing, but the comforting voice of the BBC. Why am I not surprised?"

"And what if it was your voice I was missing? Would it really make a difference?" Tookie deflected the question.

"You know, Copper, Bilkington is still well connected with the Foreign Office back home. He just might be able to land you a political position somewhere, if he were so inclined."

"You stuck the knife in deep, Tookie. Please don't twist it deeper."

"You have never understood me, Copper, after a quarter century together. That's the tragedy of us."

"Not nearly as tragic as this silly wedding you're proposing. I simply won't stand for it."

"That's the beauty of it. I don't need your blessings, do I? Not in Portugal."

"We never should have left England. You would be satisfied doing needlepoint by the fire."

"And you would be outside grunting with the pigs."

"Pigs I understand," he admitted.

"How about a drink," she proposed, desperate to change the subject.

"Only if you promise to forget all this nonsense and come back home with me, otherwise we have nothing to toast."

"We could toast to my upcoming wedding. You could agree to serve as best man."

"Best man at my own roasting! What do you take me for, an empty suit?" In a sudden fit of vengeance, Copper pitched Tookie over his shoulder, kicking and screaming, and climbed the staircase to the nearest bedroom. He threw her on the bed and began ripping off her evening gown.

"This is rape, Copper Jack! I'll have you shot at dawn!" she screamed.

"You will have to stand in line behind all the others, because I'm a very popular target these days." With Tookie partially undressed, Copper suddenly pulled away from her and retreated to the foot of the bed, feeling sorry for himself and ashamed at the same time. "By the way, tell Bustle I don't like his taste in women's clothing," he said, scowling at the gown he had just dismembered.

After finally catching her breath, Tookie managed a smile. "What about his taste in women?" Tookie's devious smile was all the invitation Copper needed. He felt twenty years younger as he mounted Tookie, entered her tenderly, almost shyly, as if this was the first time instead of the last. He waited for Tookie, holding firm inside her until she came, sharing a moment of closeness perhaps beyond any they had ever known together.

When it was over, Copper stayed there, lingering inside Tookie's soul a while longer, wallowing in his own sorrow. She was in no hurry to have him leave... When he finally left the room, she cried.

Back at the bodega, siesta dragged on and on. For some, the long afternoons became evening. Virgo succeeded in pushing Smitty deeper into his past than he had ever traveled. He recalled for Virgo how he blamed the failure of his first love affair on his own insecurity as a young writer and feeling even less secure as a lover. His first love was everything he ever dreamed of, an adolescent fantasy actually come true. He recalled calves as shapely as piano legs, nipples taut as bullets, black curly hair falling to her shoulders and nestled between her thighs, a body as brown as the earth that glistened and turned to a hue of burgundy beneath his clumsy, impassioned touch. She was forever the Dark Women of his life, without ever really being part of him.

It was much later when Smitty finally discovered the hurtful truth: she was in love with another man, the man she would eventually marry, bear a child, and finally divorce. Yet his feelings for her never changed over the years. Wherever on earth he tried to escape and every woman he embraced, the Dark Woman still claimed the measure of Smitty's heart.

"So that's who you see when you make love to me," Virgo said with a twinge of jealousy. "Should I cover myself with soot and sit under a mango tree?"

"She was Portuguese," Smitty explained.

An immigrant beauty and a struggling writer, engaged in a hot tenement house love affair in New York City. A plot for a good story he had never been able to write. She shared his bed and brought light to the dark squalor of their lives in the Big City, by painting verbal pictures of her native land in broken, but always enthusiastic English. Often they talked of returning to her Portuguese homeland together. Now, twenty years later, Smitty came to Portugal alone to try to understand, or forget, or to rediscover her in this land of dark, deep-set eyes.

Smitty looked affectionately upon the shapely body of his alabaster mistress. He knew Virgo wanted to share every aspect of his modest life, even cared to make him happy, and knew she probably could. Virgo could do everything but change his mind. "If you must go back then, please take me with you," she begged. "Why die of heartbreak like Copper Jack? Trust me. I know what it's like to wake up in the night without someone close by to touch. Touch me, Smitty," she whispered.

The day began with Smitty celebrating on his own the completion of his book. In the end, Virgo managed to add a key chapter when Smitty was forced to admit: "I love you."

"At least for today," she said wisely.

Copper returned to the bodega and found his two friends, Liz and Smitty, glued to the bar as late afternoon turned into early evening. For the three of them, their meeting was a melancholic reunion of best mates.

"Last time the three of us met like this, I ruined my new dentures," Copper recalled, trying to be upbeat and sounding beaten instead. "Now my wife is ruining me."

"The filthy trollop," Liz said under her breath.

"Watch your tongue, woman," Copper warned Liz, protective of Tookie even as he mourned.

"So why bother adding your own life to the top of the ash heap," Smitty challenged him. "Liz tells me the duel is back on again for some god-awful reason."

"Without Tookie, don't know what else to do with myself, Smitty," Copper admitted. Without asking, Liz poured Copper his customary brandy and sugar concoction and lit him a cigarette.

"I'm afraid Smitty's decided to abandon all of us as well," Liz announced, adding to the somber mood.

"Finished the book, then?" Copper asked. Smitty nodded.

"Jolly good, then. We do have something to celebrate after all," Copper suggested. "Break out the good stuff, Lizard, for our good friend, the Yank. Surely there's a deserving toast hovering not far from our lips."

Liz brought the fresh bottle, but in the aftermath of the day's dismal turn of events, no one could think of anything positive to say. Copper was flabbergasted by their silence. "Here I sit between a former history lecturer and a soon-to-be famous writer. Has the cat got both your tongues?" Copper asked. "Leave it to the pig farmer, will you?" He blew a couple of intelligent looking smoke rings into the air and somehow found the sanctity of the moment. "It seems to me the three of us have something very much in common. We all love someone who loves someone else instead."

"Which makes us resident members of the Lonely Hearts Club," Liz said sarcastically.

"No, which makes us love them all the more, unfortunately," Copper said sadly.

From the dining room, the sounds of a single mandolin began to weep as people started filing in for dinner. A soft voice followed with the fado's own unfailing story of betrayal and separation, a story from the 16th century about women dressed in black shawls standing along the shoreline, mourning together the many sailors lost at sea. The Portuguese singer closed his eyes, clinched his fists for strength and dug deep into his soul.

"Saudade," he sang, something about missing someone very much. "Saudade vai-tea embora," which Liz seemed to recognize as something about "let the blues go away."

"I've got it," Liz said triumphantly, finally raising her glass for a toast and quoting from a failing memory. "If equal affection cannot be, let the more loving one be me." Words that didn't exactly console the spirits, but Smitty and Copper raised their glasses anyway.

Under the creaky roof of the bodega, the unlikely trio toasted away the bittersweet memories of day, even allowing themselves an occasional laugh and a few drunken declarations of hope. Late evening became early morning. As long as they hung onto the moment, the future was theirs.

Liz joked about being so skinny in her old age that her panties sagged miserably at the crotch.

It was Smitty's turn to commiserate, joking about his book being sexier than the people he wrote about. Even Copper Jack joked about his upcoming duel with Bustle, leaning forward toward Liz and whispering, "How about granting a marked man his final wish?"

"How delightful," she winked. "Apparently I must be the only woman left standing," she chuckled.

When the day was finally done, the threesome climbed the lonely stairway together, not the marble steps of Millionaire Hill, but the termite-eaten clapboards of Casa Bodega. They staggered upstairs arm-in-arm for support, like a human chain protesting man's inhumanity against man. In the distance, a church bell tolled. Two storks made love in the belfry.

14

Beach of Enlightenment

Smitty studied the holes in Copper's undershirt carefully. "You're a better shot than I expected."

"Moth eaten, not bullet holes, trust me," Copper said, shaking his head in disappointment. "How did you know where to find me?" he barked.

"As your biographer, I'm supposed to know a few things about you." They seated themselves on the trunk of a nearby fallen tree. Smitty held his finished manuscript proudly under his arm. Copper emptied the shells from the chamber of his handgun. "Liz took it pretty hard when you decided to check out of your room at Casa Bodega."

"She's tough as nails, no woman tougher on this earth. She'll get over it. It's just easier this way. Besides, I missed my armchair, you know," he said, trying to crack a smile. "By the way, you have the look of someone about to take a journey."

"I've already been on a journey, Copper, thanks to you," Smitty concurred, handing Copper the manuscript. "I've written something damn good and I think you should read it." Copper gave the book back to Smitty.

"Only if you will serve as my eyes, you caught me without my reading glasses."

Smitty had lived with the book for most of a year. As he read the manuscript out loud to Copper and the words finally reached his own ears, Smitty's voice often cracked with emotion. He stumbled aimlessly through passage after passage, while Copper Jack listened intently, yet maintained the same stony face Smitty always came to expect from him.

Copper's only expression was to squint his eyes to avoid the glare of sunshine. Or was it to fight back an occasional, begrudging tear? Smitty would never know for sure. When the private reading was finally over, so was Copper's brief show of emotion. He stood up to stretch the kinks out of his joints stiff from sitting, lit a cigarette and turned the conversation back to the duel without ever commenting on the book.

"Isn't it strange," Copper asked, "that we turn our backs on each other in a duel before we turn and do each other in? At least your American gunslingers out West had the courage to look one another in the eye before drawing guns from their holsters and pulling the trigger."

"You've seen too much of America cinema, Copper. The untold lie is that we prefer ambush as a form of attack and ambush is something to worry about with Bustle. If I were you I'd be on my toes and high alert, Copper."

After a long, uncomfortable pause, Smitty grasped desperately for an alternative idea, any outcome but the inevitable. "Why don't you come back with me to the States and see my country in person?" he proposed, trying to find some way for Copper to save face and avoid the duel altogether.

Copper stared long into Smitty's eyes before shaking his head. "Thanks, Yank, but I think I'll stick around here and watch you ride off into the sunset. Like your Lone Ranger on the television, you've more than done your good deeds around here, lad," Copper acknowledged, which was as big a compliment from Copper as anyone would ever receive. For a writer like Smitty, it was extraordinarily hard to accept there was nothing more to say.

Without a single word exchanged between them about the book, Smitty turned and walked away knowing for sure he would never see Copper Jack again. It was small consolation to know they had touched one another deeply. Finally, Smitty disappeared from Copper's line of sight, as he heard the disturbing echo of gunshots in the distance.

A Portuguese servant admitted Smitty into the mansion on Millionaire Hill. Tookie was spread out comfortably across a huge sofa, drinking heavily from a bottle of gin on the table in front of her. It was obvious the former loyal visitors to Piccadilly Circus had deserted town, leaving the Fat Woman to sing alone in her new upgraded sitting room, and the chill of it all wasn't setting well with her.

"This place is far too imposing, don't you think?" she complained to Smitty. "Seems to frighten most visitors away and helps me understand why Mrs Bustle took up bird watching before flying the coop herself."

"Obviously this life is not the answer you were looking for," Smitty suggested.

"Look, Yank," she warned. "I know Copper means the world to you. But if you've come here to play Cupid, you are wasting your arrows. As you know by now, I have a heart of stone."

"You also have two men eating out of the palm of your hand. Only you have the power to persuade either one of them to call off this silly duel."

"What duel?" she asked, sounding surprised.

"Surely you know."

"Another of the pitfalls of hiding out in this mansion is I'm cut off from the usual grapevine gossip."

"Afraid this is more than gossip," Smitty insisted, not really trusting Tookie's show of ignorance. Nonetheless, he patiently explained the specific circumstances of the duel while her mind raced well ahead of his explanation.

"And you think I can somehow do something to stop this turn of events from happening?" she asked.

"Precisely, since you're the sole cause of it," Smitty said, not caring to spare Tookie the hard truth.

"Well, I'm flattered certainly. So who do you honestly think will win this duel?" she asked innocently.

"With his failing eyesight and from ten paces away, I wouldn't give Copper the chance to hit the broad side of a barn."

"He's much more of a sharp shooter than you give him credit for, Smitty. He was every bit the war hero."

"So I hear and Bustle was a big game hunter. The only point that matters is – someone very close to you is about to get seriously hurt."

"As if I'm not hurting, so who ever cares about me? Besides, getting Copper to change his mind about anything is like shifting a block of granite from one continent to the next. Good luck achieving that mission any time soon. It's been years since I've been able to penetrate his soul or influence his thinking."

"Your feeble reservations or lame excuses for sitting on your hands don't really matter. Copper's about to commit suicide and his death will be squarely on your watch because only you can prevent it."

"Look, Smitty. Copper and I have never been as close as he may have thought. Truth is I strung Copper along for ten years, not because I wanted my children grown and gone first, which was the excuse I used with Copper. Actually, I strung him out because I was secretly hoping to be swept off my feet by some Baron or Lord."

"Someone exactly like Bustle, no doubt."

She nodded and then explained. "I was an extremely attractive woman, Smitty. I had other options. Copper was my last resort. I suppose I loved him, after he agreed to sell off that detestable pig farm and generate a certain level of income and status for us, until even that wasn't enough. Problem is, I've always wanted more out of life than Copper ever needed."

"Sadly, the only thing Copper ever needed was you," Smitty said, with disgust.

"Think whatever you want, Smitty. I've been faithful to Copper ever since we got married. Maybe, later in life, it's true, I'm more pragmatic, less of a romantic. The money we got from the sale of Copper's pig farm seemed like a fortune to both of us at the time. Once we came down here as commoners and saw how all the other Brits were living, it was obvious Copper's money would not keep us in peaches and cream forever. In his mind, Copper always assumed he could go back to farming if the money ran out. Then his health took a turn for the worse, made that impossible and he started contemplating suicide. Suddenly I had to come to terms with the idea of not only growing old, but living alone and destitute. I simply couldn't bear the thought of it."

Smitty wasn't buying Tookie's justification. "But with Bustle dead, you would be back in the same predicament. So you really are rooting against your husband, aren't you?"

"Actually, Smitty, this has not been announced publicly. Bustle and I shall be married soon," she sighed, with a sense of relief. "As my new husband, Bilkington's agreed to make me legal heir to his estate. So, no matter what happens, I'll be well taken care of for the first time in my life."

"Well, congratulations, Lady Macbeth. You're not rooting for anyone but yourself because you can't lose. And if they both get shot, you collect twice. Brilliant strategy, if I must say so myself," Smitty said, making no effort to hide his anger.

"Don't make me out to be so sinister, Smitty. If Copper challenged Bustle publicly as you say, I can't very well stand in the way of two men defending their own honor, now can I?"

"You're the sole cause of the duel and you couldn't care less about either man or their honor."

"You're giving me far too much credit. Look, under the circumstances, best I can do is chat with Copper and Bilkington, perhaps convince them that fair play must prevail between gentlemen. Protocol requires a third party to witness the duel to guard against foul play. Captain Baptiste has always been a friend of the English community. For a modest fee, I'm sure the Portuguese police officer could be persuaded to referee the event."

"So you would at least give Copper a fighting chance," Smitty said, marveling at her cold, calculating ways to the bitter end. "How touching."

"I couldn't agree more," Tookie said sharply, taking solace for coming up with a solution to a problem she insisted she never masterminded.

Smitty and Virgo strolled together on the deserted beach and observed the first tell-tale signs of winter. An obese Frenchman in a white bathrobe chased futilely after his black beret, which blew off his head with the wind and was tossed into the deep blue sea. A masculine German-looking woman with evasive eyes walked by, clinging desperately to the leash of her Doberman, while trying to scoop up seashells washed ashore. Otherwise, the beach was completely vacant of the usual crowd of European vacationers. Smitty and Virgo relished winter's first curtain call all to themselves.

They walked past idle Portuguese fishing boats which, because of the threat of high tide, were strung together in colorful clusters like bouquets of flowers. As Smitty and Virgo drew near, the name of one boat caught their eye: Praia de Luz. "Beach of enlightenment," Virgo translated for Smitty, which in the end described accurately his odyssey to the Algarve, Smitty decided.

Eventually Smitty and Virgo found a dry sand dune and dropped out of sight. Smitty confided with Virgo about his meeting with Tookie, while Virgo played on Smitty's concerns in a desperate, last-ditch effort to keep Smitty from returning to the States. "So, what do you think will happen to Copper if you leave?" she asked.

"As I recall, Virgo, you read Copper's palm and already predicted the outcome. Why would I want to be around when that happens?"

"Then, what about me?" she asked Smitty for the very last time, pouting for emphasis, but getting no answer in return.

"Then I'll wait for you," she said stubbornly. "You'll be back," she predicted.

As with Copper Jack, there was nothing more Smitty could say to Virgo. He watched the cloudy winter sky somehow change the color of her eyes from brown to hazel. The pullover sweater she wore to brace herself against the wind made her look younger and more vulnerable.

They spent their last afternoon together in Portugal sitting back-to-back like bookends, with no desire to speak or even look into each other's eyes. As romantic farewells unfold, this one wasn't much to remember. Their skin tingled quietly beneath their warm clothes. Chests heaved and fell heavily with the tide. Heads tilted back to rest on one another's shoulders and to look upon the gray and troubled sky above. Their hearts, like the ocean waves crashing around them, grew darker and pounded relentlessly inside their breasts.

15

Do Not Go Gentle into That Good Night

With Tookie and Smitty now removed from the picture frame, the arrival of another winter season unsettled Copper's nerves. To fend off the chill, he drank brandy like it was water and wore socks beneath his cotton slippers. Like his undershirt full of bullet holes, his socks were moth-eaten and would go without mending. Because some things in life simply can't be repaired, or aren't worth it anyway.

The fire in the fireplace kept sputtering and dying out. His only spiritual support came from the thread-thin arms of his beloved armchair, which rose up in his time of need to envelop him like great pillars of strength. To break the deadly silence of an otherwise empty house, Copper sought out the companionship of his own scratchy voice. Smitty spawned the bright idea of having Copper record his private thoughts, but Copper never felt comfortable talking into a machine. Now there was no one else he could talk to. So without hesitation, he pushed the button on the tape recorder and spoke to no one in particular.

"Copper Jack here," he began, stopping the tape immediately and reversing it to hear how he sounded. "Copper Jack here," the machine repeated stiffly.

Now what, he wondered? He could think of nothing to say that would be memorable. Copper focused on a lonely ember burning low in the fireplace. *Click*: "Remember my lame story, Smitty, about throwing another log on the fire? Or did I even tell you that story? My mind's all mush. Anyway, in case you were wondering, it's time to throw another log on." *Click*...

Copper threw a log on the fire and, after a few pokes, he felt the warmth return.

Click: "Copper Jack here again, warm as toast this time. If you wonder, Smitty, why I finally decided to make this personal recording, it's because I started talking to myself and it worried me. So far at least, I finally fancy this little gargle box you left behind for me. Best thing is, it doesn't talk back to me like a woman," he laughed out loud: *Click*.

Click: "Finally spoke with Tookie. After all these years, she's decided she's too rich for my blood, imagine that? She's after Bustle's pocketbook, not his pecker. Says she still loves me, but saying it that way doesn't sound very sincere." *Click*.

Click: "Not to worry, though, I'll cope somehow. That's what I do. And it won't be long now. I even hit the target I was shooting at in practice today. Fingers crossed." *Click*.

Click: "About your book, Smitty, as you know, I am no educated man. But what you read to me, I think you are on to something very big. In everything you say about love, you are spot on, lad. You got it right. However, the old man in your story, the main character I guess and given his good looks, he should have been much more of a womanizer, don't you think, especially if we're considering a motion picture someday?" *(Loud cackle from Copper)*

"You know, after the war, I promised myself I would visit at least one veteran every year, to cheer him up a bit, if I could. Make him laugh and feel better for a few minutes, as every vet should be allowed. Kind of my personal thanks for returning from the war in one piece when so many of my buddies did not. No one around here seems to remember what a real fighting war was like. You were someone I could talk to, Yank." *Click*.

Click: "When I was a small kid in Kent, I remember the ice-man came around every day with a fresh block of ice for the kitchen fridge. And then there was the baker, the butcher, the milkman and the postman all appearing magically on our doorstep each and every day with everything our family needed to be happy. Life seemed so much simpler then.

"I used to sit in this armchair for hours and hear nothing but the precise gears turning over in my mind. Now the gears get stuck, don't turn as often. And when they do, they sometimes replay something I would just as well like to forget. Like, in my mind, I still hear Tookie breathing easily in her sleep just down the hallway from my armchair." *Click*.

Click: "Saw Liz the other day. You remember Liz, Smitty. Complained she didn't know whether to order flowers to decorate the bodega for a wedding for Tookie or a funeral for me. Told her she and Reverend Pat wouldn't have to bother about a funeral on my account. My will calls for my ashes to be dumped at sea without ceremony when the time comes. I always respected the greatest natural force in Nature and I owe Neptune a soul or two from the war when I snatched death from his jaws more than I deserved." *Click*.

Click: "I have some regrets, Yank. Your parents die and a million loving words come to mind you should have said and didn't while they were alive and always at your side. Same thing when your marriage ends out of the blue. Or a best friend like you suddenly decides to leave. Sometimes I think it would be nice to have your life back again, like one of these audio tapes, so you can erase it all and do it proper next time around." *Click.*

It was a proper church wedding this time, no sneaking about the altar as Tookie and Copper had resorted to in Kent many years ago. This time Tookie was elegantly dressed and properly blessed.

"Do you, Tookie, take Bilkington as your lawful wedded husband?" Reverend Pat asked.

"I do," she said, without a quiver of betrayal in her voice.

"Do you, Bilkington, take Tookie as your lawful wedded wife?"

"I do."

"Then, with the powers vested in this church, I pronounce you man and wife."

Bustle pressed against Tookie an interminable kiss, holding up the spoils of victory for all the bodega brethren to witness. As the couple turned finally and headed slowly back down the aisle of matrimony together, Bustle beamed from ear-to-ear and back again. Tookie surrendered a smile, but her eyes glistened as she and Bustle passed by her very own Copper Jack. Tookie thought she might have caught a forgiving nod from him in return, even as Copper bit into his lip with remorse. Once Tookie and Bustle vanished into the crowd, Copper and Liz locked arms and trailed the newlyweds down the aisle. Copper leaned heavily on Liz's unsteady ninety pounds of weight for support.

Copper agreed to serve as best man for one inexplicable reason: in his heart, he believed the vows Tookie swore to honor until death were directed to him, not Bustle. In his wildest dreams, he even thought she might change her mind at the very last instant and he would be there waiting to forgive her. Unfortunately, he had been an old sentimental fart to the bitter end. Liz whispered encouragement in his ear.

"Though lovers be lost, love shall not," she said, as if these words were supposed to cheer him up. What Liz didn't bother to tell Copper was the poet that wrote this sentiment lost both, his lover and love, before losing his mind entirely.

The wedding reception at Casa Bodega was vintage Sunday Slosh, with equal parts drinking and dancing. Dining room tables were cleared to make room for a proper dance floor. A Portuguese band serenaded the bride and groom with love songs. Bustle led Tookie around the dance floor masterfully in the traditional first dance. Copper butted in at the start of the second. "Admirable, old chap, how you can be such a sport about this wedding," Bustle gushed, before stepping aside, handing over his new wife, and racing to the bar without hesitation.

As couples suddenly cleared the dance floor, Copper was impervious to everyone at the bodega except Tookie. He was not a natural dancer and always resisted Tookie's coaching tips, despite the bruised feet he inflicted upon her. Once again, he couldn't resist his favorite line when, true to form, his first dance step landed squarely upon her toes.

"They should tie us together like cattle with a rope around our ankles, so you could follow me better than you do," he laughed. It was an endearment he always used to excuse his poor dancing technique. This time Tookie didn't seem to mind. She laughed along with Copper and tried to follow along with her silver-haired war hero as best she could.

"Recognize the suit I'm wearing?" Copper asked, referring to his old wedding suit.

"Like you, your old wedding suit has seen better days," Tookie admitted. Gradually, the dance floor filled up again with other couples. Copper and Tookie danced silently and closely for several more numbers. Tookie used these magical moments from the past to reflect upon her recent decisions, not to regret them.

"Copper," she said suddenly. "We're not moving."

"Time should stand so still," he said, shuffling his feet once again to the music.

When Bustle finally returned to the dance floor, more than fortified from his trip to the bar, Copper showed no inclination to step aside.

"Copper, please, don't do this," she pleaded, sensing the potential for provocation but Copper couldn't or wouldn't turn her loose and Bustle was clearly miffed. It was Tookie who finally twisted free.

"I was willing to forgive and forget, old sport," Bustle said, reeking of alcohol. "I saw, in your willingness to serve as best man, a willingness to bury the hatchet, but obviously Tookie will never be mine free and clear without a fight. I'll anchor my yacht offshore within a fortnight. I'll be alone with two pistols. If you're half a man, you'll be there."

"I'll not only be there, I'll be the best man again," Copper assured him smugly.

The wedding reception progressed without further incident. Frill Pimpton managed to make a spectacle of herself as expected. The festivities ended appropriately with Liz filling up Copper's glass and ego at the end of the bar.

"Start preparing the bodega for Bustle's funeral," Copper exclaimed with bravado.

"You are twice the man he is, Copper Jack. If there were more men like you, there would be less like his sort. You have nothing to prove. You know how I feel about you. I must say I don't find this death-wish of yours especially attractive."

"And what other choice do I have, Lizard?"

"Just give the word, and this well-preserved woman on the other side of the bar is all yours. After the wedding, the Reverend leaves town for another wedding in Portimao. Why not stay the night?"

"In my mind, I'm going to my grave as Tookie's husband and your best friend," he added. "What can possibly be better?" He reached for his wallet to pay for an evening of drinks and conversation, but Liz would hear none of it.

"You will always owe me. Count on it."

Copper left the bodega as loneliness closed in on Liz like death itself. The solitude Smitty found productive for writing was the source of her gradual unraveling. Liz carried in her breast an emptiness she could no longer fill with laughter or drink into oblivion. Copper was the final, unwilling thread holding her life together.

Liz finished washing up around the bar, downed a final nightcap for good measure and climbed the stairway all alone. At the top of the stairs, she passed her room and continued to the end of the hallway. She knocked at Virgo's door out of habit, but there was no answer. Liz entered the room, noticed Virgo's black bag of tricks and wondered if she could do herself a good turn.

Tookie recalled her previous wedding day in Kent with mixed emotions. It began with a rushed wedding ceremony with a drunken local pastor who they pulled out of bed at the crack of dawn. Immediately after the hurried ceremony, she and Copper traveled most of the day in the caravan with no specific destination in mind. They eventually ran out of petrol and checked into a cheap hotel in some forgotten French village.

Besides a bed, what they wanted most was a bath which they found at the end of the hallway to be shared with all the other hotel occupants. When they entered their bedroom and Tookie found a pair of nylons left over from the previous one-night stand, she remembered feeling unclean and slept alone that first night of marriage, much to Copper's dismay.

"Why such a long face on our wedding night, my dearest?" Bustle asked, entering her bedroom and interrupting her thoughts. Bustle wore a smart looking smoking jacket and a splash of fresh cologne in hopes of finally getting his new bride into bed.

"Worried about this ghastly duel, I guess."

"Worried about Copper, you mean," Bustle replied, sounding smitten.

"Worried about you, of course," she corrected him, "and about me, if anything should happen to you, God forbid."

"My dear, rest your mind. You are taken care of, as promised. You will share my wealth and the wealth of my dearly departed brother's estate as well."

"So, it's all settled then, Bilkington?" Tookie said, perking up suddenly.

"We are one," he reassured her, "at least on paper."

"What a delightful wedding present! You have no idea the peace of mind you have given me for the first time in my life," she said, taking Bustle's hand and placing it against her breast. "I would feel even better if we took steps to protect your safety. I don't care to be a widow."

"Do not worry your pretty little head, Tookie. Copper doesn't stand a chance."

"I know Copper better than you do. He can be quite devious, you know."

"So can I."

"How so?"

"By cutting my ten paces a few steps short," he smiled.

"What makes you certain Copper won't do the same?"

"Because we all know Copper Jack's a right honorable fellow."

"Still, perhaps I should come along as a witness in case something goes wrong. As you know, protocol requires a third party to be present."

"I won't hear of it. It's not proper for a lady."

"Then how about hiring Captain Baptiste? He's flirted with me on occasion. I am sure we can arrange for Baptiste to keep a wary eye on Copper."

"Simply doesn't sound like the Copper I know but if it will settle your mind, so be it. But what makes you so sure Copper will go along with it?"

"I'll make sure he does," she promised.

Tookie turned to Bustle and helped him to his feet. She decided he was starting to look too comfortable in her bedroom. "Now, if you will excuse me, Bilkington. A new bride needs her sleep. It has been an exhausting wedding day."

"This is preposterous," he objected. "They would laugh me out of the Club if it were discovered I spent my wedding night begging for sex outside your doorstep like a puppy dog!"

"Our little secret," she tried to console him. "In a fortnight when this duel is behind us, I'll be all yours," she promised.

After Bustle stormed off into the night, Tookie opted for a self-satisfied stroll to the balcony before bedtime. It was a cold October night, not a night to be alone; yet the dim luster of Copper's reading light in the distance, burning a hole in the darkness at the bottom of Millionaire Hill, warmed her blood and strengthened her spine for the task ahead of her.

16

Rage, Rage Against the Dying of the Light

Nothing much had changed in Copper Jack's sitting room, yet something important was missing. Tookie surveyed the familiar surroundings with consternation. Even when they both lived under the same roof, the parlor never seemed quite orderly unless Copper Jack and his armchair anchored his side of the fireplace. Suddenly, Tookie realized what bothered her: the gaping emptiness on her side of the fireplace. Her armchair had somehow disappeared!

"I donated your chair to our maid as a reward for her many years of thankless, dedicated service," Copper said, entering from the hallway and passing Tookie on the way to his armchair. "Besides, I suddenly found myself talking to the chair as if you were still sitting there. Not good, especially when the chair itself talked back to me, that's when I knew it had to go," he said, forcing a smile and pouring two brandies.

"Actually, I came here looking for you, Copper, not my armchair," she said, trying hard not to show her disappointment.

"Hope you haven't come to try to change things. What's done is done," he mimicked her, throwing her own words back at her from their most recent encounter.

"You certainly don't make me feel sorry I left you."

"If I could make you feel anything, now that would be a miracle," he said, handing her a glass of brandy which Tookie promptly slapped from his hand. Glass shattered on the floor in the vicinity of her missing armchair.

"Guess I'll just have to drink alone then," he mumbled, easing into his armchair as if nothing remarkable had just happened. Tookie was left to sit alone on the sofa.

"I came here today to warn you, Copper, Bustle's simply not to be trusted when you turn your back on him."

"You knew that before you married him."

"I didn't marry Bustle for the same reasons I married you. I still care about you."

"I won't be talked out of the duel, Tookie. And don't flatter yourself. At this point, I'm doing it for myself, not for you," he assured her.

"But I don't understand. You swore off all violence of any kind following the war. You said you'd lost your stomach for fighting."

"I stand to lose more than my stomach this time."

"That's why I've come, to save you from yourself."

The old spark flared up momentarily in Copper's gut. His eyes twinkled and a shitty little grin escaped from the corners of his mouth. He poured Tookie another brandy which she accepted this time and he sat close to her on the sofa.

"I notice you said 'that's why I've come' not 'that's why I've come back'."

"That's because I'm not coming back, Copper. I'm married, remember? You were the best man."

Copper finished off his brandy without taking a breath, left Tookie's side at the sofa and slumped back into his armchair across the room.

"Then damn your concerns," he said finally.

Tookie's eyes began to well up in tears. Her throat tightened before blurting out, "I miss my bloody armchair and feel at a distinct disadvantage without it," she confessed.

Once again, Copper pulled himself reluctantly out of the armchair and joined Tookie on the sofa, trying to console her. "Once upon a time, a healthy blow up like this was good for sex," he said, almost whispering to himself.

Tookie drank the brandy, holding the glass with two hands and gulping it in one swig, like strong medicine. With Copper at her side and suddenly feeling sympathetic to her cause, she decided it was time to broach the subject of having Captain Baptiste present at the duel – for Copper's sake, she told him.

Copper set aside his glass and drank in the moment instead. With Tookie once again at his side, voicing what sounded like sincere concern about his welfare, life suddenly seemed worth living again.

"Maybe that's where you and I went wrong," Copper teased. "Instead of separate armchairs, maybe we should have sat side-by-side on the sofa all those years together," he smiled.

"So, you agree Captain Baptiste can preside over the duel?" Tookie asked.

"I'm not even sure we need a duel if you and I can still share private moments like this as good friends," Copper suggested.

Suddenly Tookie realized her mission was overly successful. On her return to Millionaire Hill, she needed to devise another plot to make sure Copper realized she was worth dying for once again.

Tookie's telephone call the next morning found Copper brooding in his armchair. Her visit reminded him how alone he was in the world without her. The sound of her voice over the telephone was the elixir he needed to brighten up his day. When she also invited him to lunch at the mansion, he felt his heart miss a beat in anticipation.

"Bustle will be at the Club all day long, so I thought we could continue our conversation over lunch," she proposed.

"I'll be there with bells on," he promised.

Bilkington Bustle found himself cornered in Tookie's bedroom suite shortly before he was to tee off at the Club.

"I'll never be permitted on the golf course again if I leave them waiting," he said, pleasantly surprised by Tookie's sudden amorous ways.

The satin sheets on the bed were pulled back purposefully. A silver tray with an open bottle of champagne stood waiting at the bedside. The French doors to the balcony were thrown wide open, allowing the curtains to capture the ocean breezes and billow forth into the bedroom dramatically. Tookie tossed aside her bathrobe and leaned back on the bed wearing a suggestive, free-flowing nightgown which left very little to the imagination.

"To what do I attribute my sudden good fortune," Bustle asked, with a slightly puzzled look on his face.

"We are husband and wife, remember?"

"I've been waiting for it to dawn on you," Bustle reminded her.

"Maybe I'm tired of sharing you with Frill Pimpton. You don't expect me to believe you spend every day chasing golf balls, do you?" she said, pulling Bustle on top of her.

By the time Copper reached Millionaire Hill at the appointed hour, the Portuguese maid waved him up the spiral staircase without hesitation. Copper didn't bother to knock on the bedroom door because the maid assured him Tookie was expecting him but, when he entered the room, he found Bustle's bare ass thrust into the air humping away madly and heard Tookie's muffled groans of pleasure beneath him.

It was left to his dear friend Liz to administer last rites. Like a wounded soldier, Copper stumbled into the crowded bodega during siesta, mumbling deliriously to himself, and not knowing where else to turn. Liz motioned for Reverend Pat to tend to her customers while she guided Copper safely to the end of the bar where they could talk. She poured brandy down his gullet until Copper finally started to make some sense.

"Did I hear you say the duel's tomorrow?" Liz asked.

"The sun won't rise soon enough," Copper confided.

"The filthy trollop."

For once, Copper did not refute Liz's color commentary on Tookie's total lack of character. Not since the war had Copper burned this deeply in the bowels, a burning he would live with until dawn when he could finally do something about it. Liz spent the remainder of the afternoon trying to console Copper, perhaps even change his mind but when he finished his last drink, he put money on the counter and insisted she bank the proceeds this time.

"You know I can't promise I'll be back, Lizard."

Dawn broke over the early horizon, casting long shadows against a backdrop of green clover and sorrel covering the slope of Portuguese hillsides in winter. Fresh laundry from the village clotheslines flapped madly in the wind as dark eyes peered out from behind half-open window shutters. The church bell peeled softly as Mr Bom Dia assumed a sitting position on his favorite neighborhood doorstep.

Copper Jack stopped his car long enough to share a cigarette with Mr Bom Dia and a nip from his brandy bottle to build up his courage. Together they greeted the fishermen who passed by en route to the market, carrying with them their hard-earned catch salvaged during a sleepless night navigating rough and unforgiving Atlantic seas.

When Copper's car finally reached the harbor reluctantly, he found Captain Baptiste waiting patiently for him in a rowboat. If the cold wind didn't wake you up, the smell of ripe sewage in shallow water would do the trick. The Captain rowed the boat while Copper Jack gazed back on the Portuguese village receding in the distance, trying to fix the scene forever in his mind. From a distance, everything in his vision soon became blurry except for the village laundry held perfectly stiff in the wind, like somber flags at half-mast.

The Captain grunted as he rowed. Each tug of the oars pulled savagely at Copper's insides. He grew weak and pale as the ocean waves rocked the boat and he hung his head over the side to spill the contents of his stomach into the sea. His insides were completely empty by the time the rowboat pulled up alongside the yacht.

Towering above him, Copper saw Bilkington Bustle strutting around the deck of the yacht freshly shaved, alert and chipper than ever. He slapped his arms against his body like a penguin to stay warm. The psychological advantage was clearly on Bustle's side as Tookie stepped out of the cabin and joined Bustle in a show of solidarity. Copper had not expected Tookie to be there and would have preferred never to see her again.

As they reached the deck of the yacht together, Captain Baptiste helped steady Copper until he found his sea legs. The yacht swayed gently to and fro, while everyone nodded in silence and moved in slow motion as if in a dream. Finally, the Captain took care of the particulars. He armed each competitor with loaded pistols and aligned them back-to-back before withdrawing to a safer distance and motioning for Tookie to do the same.

Copper cocked his right arm in the air and held the gun steady well above his shoulder, pointed skyward. The beat of his heart was thunderous. Before Captain Baptiste gave the signal to begin, Copper found Tookie out of the corner of his eye. He looked for some sign that the duel would commence against her will, instead of with her blessings. Instead, she had already turned her back on the proceedings, not wanting to watch the outcome. Like soldiers at the warfront, Copper no longer remembered the valiant cause for which he was fighting.

Captain Baptiste gave the signal to begin. Copper's first measured step felt like he was falling into a bottomless pit toward a fate he no longer controlled. The foolishness of killing and dying from the war came back to him with a rush. In a few condensed seconds, all would be revealed.

Copper's second and third steps were more resolute as his survival instincts started to kick in. By his fourth step he was breathing normally, almost serenely, ready to face death with the same stony cheek he had turned to life's hardships along the way.

By his fifth step, Copper's vision began to blur from the sweat pouring from his brow into his eyes. A moment of panic swept over him, a premonition perhaps. Before he could take another step, he was hit in the back by a force which knocked him to his knees, as if in prayer. At that exact instant, Captain Baptiste fired a retaliatory shot, bringing Bustle to his knees.

Unfortunately the Captain's bullet was too late to help Copper Jack, as he slumped face down in a pool of his own blood. A heavy weight and physical presence suddenly covered the full length of Copper's body, pressing against him with what used to be a life-saving force that had sustained him many times before. Copper would carry to his grave the memory of Tookie Jack's hot tears raining down unabashedly against the back of his neck. Her screams could be heard above the ocean din as if something had gone terribly wrong.

Following the deadly duel on the yacht, with blood on her hands and her conscience, Tookie Jack was so overcome with grief she jumped overboard before Captain Baptiste could restrain her. Only Virgo and Smitty were spared a ghastly outcome.

Epilogue

For the next few days, Virgo was content to serve as his tour guide and Smitty was just as happy to follow her lead as she showed off her homeland, this famous island playground of the bards. Perhaps in the extremities the Empire had grown decadent, unwieldy and come unstuck all together. Still, at the heart of London, it was the same country of Copper Jack's childhood.

For hours on end, Smitty and Virgo wandered arm-in-arm through the idyllic city parks, pausing along the crowded boulevards to sip tea and nibble cheese scones, never tiring of the gently spitting skies above. Inevitably, such impressionable scenery brought them back to themselves.

"You rarely talk about your writing, Smitty, even though it means the world to you," Virgo said, breaking the silence between them.

"Or about making love," Smitty noted, "because some things need to be felt, not discussed."

"So what are you feeling at the moment?"

"As if I'm about to start an entirely new chapter in my life."

Virgo nodded to show she understood Smitty, even if she didn't. She looked out under the canvas awning where they took momentary shelter from the weather, and watched the steady drizzle as it puddled on the cobblestone walkway.

"As for myself, I forgot how lovely life can be," she said, taking Smitty's hand and leading him to their next destination.

To get out of the rain for a while, they boarded a red double-decker bus for a guided tour of the city. The tour guide pointed to sites with names Smitty recalled from history books: Westminster Abbey, the Houses of Parliament and Buckingham Palace – all the many famous monuments of English history. However, once the bus turned the corner at Hyde Park, the exalted landmarks of Church and State gradually gave way to a tawdry roundabout overrun with annoying billboards, bright neon signs and the smell of fish and chips everywhere you turned.

"Piccadilly Circus," the guide announced suddenly. "You are looking upon the heart of London's theater and market districts, also a favorite gathering place for pigeons and curious tourists like yourselves. No doubt you are all here to seek out our infamous peep shows and street pimps," he joked. Since no one seemed to be in a laughing mood, the tour guide became serious again. "As we pass by the traffic island, you will notice a bronze fountain anchoring the middle of the roundabout and the statue, looking as if he's directing the busy traffic jam, is Eros, Greek god of love, passion and compassion.

"According to legend, Eros is actually responsible for directing the course of our innermost human desires. Speaking of desires, this brings us to the red-light district of Soho – an entirely different legend of sorts."

At the end of their time together in London, Virgo was blunt with Smitty: "So you can see why I can't possibly go home to the States with you. For me, this will always be home." It didn't really matter that Smitty had not invited her to America in the first place. This was simply Virgo's gentle way of letting him off the hook politely and relieving Smitty of the melodrama of having to walk out on her. Smitty was now free to resume his pursuit of the Dark Woman in his life and, because of Virgo and Copper Jack he could resume his chase, a better man than before.

"You know where to find me, Yank, if you get tired of chasing shadows," Virgo smiled. "It's all in the palm of your hand."

The End

James Allen Mitchell

James began his career in his twenties teaching creative writing, before resigning to travel to Europe to write 'the next great American novel'. After a year abroad, he ran out of money and returned to the States with a one-hundred page draft he would complete years later. In the meantime, he launched a career as an executive speechwriter and wrote for executives at four different corporations, the last being IBM.

At IBM, James Allen Mitchell served as an executive speechwriter and magazine publisher, before becoming a corporate communications executive. As an executive, he worked on assignment in Paris for more than three years. Not until he retired from IBM did he rewrite *Piccadilly Circus*, the novel he began in Portugal almost 40 years earlier.

Since retiring from IBM, he has also written two other novels: a literary romance that takes place in Manhattan and Paris and is based loosely on his own experience as a publisher, and a third novel based on his childhood in Oklahoma and his teenage years in California.

James and his wife live in Connecticut where they raised two sons and now enjoy the company of a grandson.

www.ingramcontent.com/pod-product-compliance
Lightning Source LLC
Chambersburg PA
CBHW082033170626
46817CB00010B/3145